Jungle Sunrise

Praise for Jonathan Williams' Novel

Jungle Sunrise is a unique and captivating novel, written by a member of the Xtreme Team, an inimitable group of men and women who risk their lives and endure unthinkable physical deprivation while attempting to find and assist native people in the most remote areas of the world. Author Jonathan Williams has written this novel out of the rich background of that experience. He unlocks the secret of how to begin life anew, as the book's central character moves from a depressing, directionless life to a rewarding and incomparable adventure. One warning: do not start reading until you have some time because you won't put it down.

— Paige Patterson
President, Southwestern Baptist Theological Seminary

Jonathan Williams skillfully transports the reader between two worlds in a captivating and suspenseful book. Having traveled in this setting with young missionaries seeking to reach isolated jungle tribes, I can attest to the authenticity of experiences encountered in this rich yet challenging environment. It is evident the author has been there! A subtle Christian testimony is effectively woven into the novel through intriguing personalities as they discover the ultimate meaning in life through trials and tragedy.

— Jerry Rankin
President, International Mission Board, SBC

A NOVEL

JONATHAN WILLIAMS

Noble
Novels

VENTURA, CALIFORNIA
2010

JUNGLE SUNRISE

published by  a division of

Copyright © 2010 by Jonathan Williams

ISBN: 978-0-9824929-8-7

Library of Congress Control Number 2010902112

Editor, Kimberley Winters Woods

Cover and Interior Design, Desta Garrett

Cover Photo, Jonathan Williams

Proofreader, Mary Malcolm

Jungle Sunrise is a work of fiction. All names, characters, places, and incidents are the products of the author's imagination or are used fictitiously. Any resemblance to current events or locales, or to real persons living or dead, is entirely coincidental.

Printed in the United States of America

NORDSKOG PUBLISHING, INC.
2716 Sailor Ave., Ventura, California 93001 USA
1-805-642-2070 • 1-805-276-5129
www.NordskogPublishing.com

Member,

Christian Small Publishers Association

For the love of my life,
Jess.
You inspire creativity, reflect God's beauty,
and make this adventurous journey
unsurpassable.
With you, I'm always "downriver."

PART ONE

Coconut Juice
and
Whiskey

CHAPTER 1

MEMPHIS gripped his four-foot-long wooden bow in his left hand as he knelt on one knee behind the thick brush. Two hand-carved arrows, as long as the bow, leaned against the trunk of a tree just a few inches away. Sweat from his hairline ran through the dry mud on his forehead and into his eyes. An orange sun peeked into the jungle foliage from the edge of the horizon, and Memphis's body began to feel the wear of the two-hour wait.

Although he could not even slightly hear or see him, Memphis knew that Artone endured the same exhaustion nearby. Memphis shifted his weight without making a sound or flinching from his fixed stare set on the shallow pool of fresh water twenty feet in front of his shield of bushes. His parched lips, dry throat, and unquenched thirst begged him to run and dunk his head into the clear pool.

Memphis dipped his right index finger into the open coconut sitting on the ground by his calloused bare feet. Running the wet finger over his tongue and lips, he enjoyed the last drops of the coconut milk, one of the few amenities of the Peruvian Amazon jungle.

I should be good for another half hour he thought, shifting his kneeling stance to his left knee.

Memphis heard a small stick break. He froze. He knew his movement had not caused the sound. There were no limbs lying in the spot where he waited, for he had cleared out all debris when he settled in the night before. Something else had snapped the twig. A pile of leaves rustled. Another cracking of a stick sounded.

Memphis slowly reached for an arrow, his eyes fixed on the clearing between his hideout and the pond. By the time the jaguar stepped out of the forest and into the clearing, the arrow rested firmly against the taut rope and wood of Memphis's bow, the point aimed a few feet in front of the approaching cat.

The young male flaunted black spots artfully painted across his yellow canvas. His long tail swayed like the body of a dancer as he strode toward the water. Threat rode on his shoulders. Fierceness lived in his eyes. His walk seemed prideful and fearless as if he were fully aware of his wildness and strength.

For a moment, Memphis forgot that he was the hunter.

It was agreed that Artone, the more experienced hunter and, by rule, the better shot, would make the first move. Memphis followed the unsuspecting prey with the tip of his arrow. The bowstring lined Memphis's palm, ready for release.

He's all yours, Art, Memphis thought to himself. Just pull your arrow back to your cheek and fire that thing right into his neck.

Memphis could picture Artone tucked away out there, hidden in the dense jungle. Some lingering dew rolled off a leaf onto Memphis's head as he attempted to will his friend into action.

Come on, Art! Catch us some dinner.

The young jaguar continued on a steady, predictable path. He methodically closed in on the pond. At just a stone's throw away, however, the jaguar hesitated momentarily, just enough to escape the unforeseen arrow.

Artone's shot ripped through some high weeds across the clearing from Memphis and severed the jaguar's left ear. Immediately, the wounded animal streaked away. Simultaneously, Memphis and Artone exploded out of the brush and into the clearing. Arrow still drawn, Memphis raced into the jungle, following the bloodstained trail. Artone lifted his spear high as he chased after a second chance.

"*Mente? Mente?*" Memphis shouted, having lost sight of the jaguar.

"*Keyo!*" Artone yelled as he pointed to their right.

Zigzagging through the trees, the two men sprinted over logs, under limbs, and through thorns that promised pain to come. Artone split off to Memphis's left up onto a ridge that afforded him a view of the entire area. He now ran parallel to Memphis, only ten feet higher.

Drumming feet echoed through the jungle and Memphis caught a glimpse of the jaguar. He narrowed in on the sound of his steps. Just when he thought he had pinpointed the direction of the sound, another noise from behind broke his concentration.

Memphis slowed his pace and listened to differentiate the sounds. His confused ears failed him and he decided to keep tracking in his current direction. As he hurdled a cluster of exposed roots, his adrenalin racing as fast as his legs were moving, he turned to see the male jaguar running straight for him.

Memphis could see Artone running directly behind the beast down the small ridge adjacent to the hunting ground. Memphis knelt on one knee, pulled his arrow back, and aimed at the jaguar, a mere twenty-five yards away and closing quickly. In a weak attempt to calm his nerves, Memphis breathed in deeply and then slowly exhaled.

Artone flew off the hill onto level ground racing against the rapidly approaching showdown. Chasing the jaguar as the jaguar charged Memphis, Artone launched his spear. The jaguar leaped and the spear missed its target, sliding across the jungle floor toward Memphis. Without flinching, Memphis released a true arrow. The jaguar fell at his killer's feet with one ear missing and an arrow protruding through his upper-body.

Before Memphis could breathe again, Artone cried out Memphis's native nickname, "Budteré! Budteré!" Running toward Memphis hysterically with his arms waving around as if he were trying to fly, Artone desperately tried to warn his friend.

Startled, Memphis peered over his shoulder in time to witness the single most fearful sight life had yet to present him. Another larger cat bore down on him, her eyes intently locked on her prey.

Filled with dread, Memphis struggled to pull the arrow from the first jaguar. Unable to dislodge the weapon, he turned, trembling with fear and helplessness, to see the object of his fright. As he did, Memphis noticed Artone's spear lying next to a tree halfway between the jaguar and himself.

Like a madman, Memphis darted for the spear. He reached it only a blink before the jaguar and, sliding leg-first, grabbed the spear, setting the dull end against the base of the tree. He erected it just as the snarling hunter leapt for the kill – mouth agape – and swallowed the point of the spear.

The spear's end protruded through the jaguar's neck, lifting

her nearly straight up before the weight of the beast flipped the spear over backwards, slamming the dying animal to the ground. Its thrashing quickly ceased, leaving nothing more than a lifeless carcass just behind the tree where Memphis sat in shock.

CHAPTER 2

*T*HE melodious chimes of nearby church bells danced throughout the city before penetrating Jonah's bedroom window like uninvited beams of sunlight in the early morning. Jonah cursed the obnoxious invasion, wishing he were deaf. If he could afford to move, he would.

Holding his pounding head, Jonah slithered out of his bed and into the bathroom where he splashed cold water on his face, ignoring the hand towel hanging next to the sink. Still wearing his jeans and shoes from the night before, he had slept – or, better put – passed out in his clothes, and was, therefore, already halfway dressed for work. Jonah put on a long-sleeve, wrinkled blue dress shirt, the same shirt he had worn to work the day before.

He stumbled into the kitchen where he put on a fresh pot of coffee. Plopping into one of the chairs at the kitchen table, Jonah pulled his laptop computer to face him and exhaled a deep sigh. He clicked the space bar and, out of habit, looked out the window while the computer woke up. His seat afforded him a modest view of the usually crowded downtown. At five in the morning, however, a strange mix of midnight shadows and morning glow pervaded the relatively lonely streets. The city that never sleeps did seem to nap at least occasionally. A feeling of solitude gently subdued Jonah.

Without enthusiasm, he opened the Microsoft Word program on his computer and proceeded to click through a series of questions. New document? Yes. Blank Document? Yes. He soon found himself staring at the familiar, depressing sight of a blank screen. The cursor blinking at the top left corner of the page taunted him. He impatiently waited for the distraction of his coffee.

A minute later, the green light on the coffee maker lit up.

Jonah gladly left his anxiety at the computer and set the coffee pot on a potholder on the counter. He opened a bottle of Irish whiskey and filled his mug two-thirds full. Adding a teaspoon of raw sugar and a small amount of hot coffee, Jonah stirred his drink with a dirty spoon and then returned to the computer. Within a half hour, he had finished three mugs of his special blend of Irish coffee, though failed to type a single word.

Instead, he had watched an old man down the street sprinkle salt on the front steps of a used bookshop. He had also changed the screensaver on his computer several times and canvassed the area below his apartment balcony with his blood-shot eyes, wishing he could skip work. And not for the first time, he wondered why the 100-year-old church next door insisted on ringing those dreadful bells every morning. For thirty minutes, Jonah sat and thought and dreamed and regretted and drank, but he had not, even once, typed.

Jonah Frost's writer's block had lasted nearly three years.

Exactly 1,070 days had passed since Jonah last wrote anything worth keeping. That short story won a first prize of

$500 from a local Barnes & Noble bookstore's grand opening competition. The short story, which painted a rather depressing picture of the endless despair of the process of divorce, was later published in a limited-circulation *Writer's Journal.* Two weeks later, Jonah's own divorce became final and he committed himself to writing his First Great Novel. In his mind, Jonah always referred to his ongoing work as his First Great Novel, for he remained confident that many more would follow.

Despite his confidence, though, there Jonah sat, alone in his apartment, trying desperately to look at anything but the blank computer screen. It might as well be a paperweight for all the use he put it to, Jonah often thought. For most writers, a three-year drought without a publishing contract would ruin any respectable reputation he had once earned among the sort of people that decide reputations. And it would most certainly rob that person of the right to say, "I'm a writer," when asked, "So, what do you do?"

It was different for Jonah, though. Not only was he the son of the late, acclaimed novelist, James Frost – author of two books mentioned by critics in conversations about recent classics, Jonah had also accumulated for himself a number of prestigious awards and accomplishments: published at age fifteen, recipient of the Young Writer's Seal two years later, the only writer under the age of twenty to be included in *America's Best Short Story Anthology,* winner of absolutely every fiction contest at NYU for four consecutive years, published in more than forty respectable short-story literary magazines, second-place winner in the annual New York City Hemingway Contest, and first place in the Barnes & Noble competition. As if all this did not prove sufficient to secure Jonah Frost a seat at the table of up-and-coming brilliant writers, his senior class in high school had named him Most Likely to Make the *New York Times* Best Seller List.

Consequently, the fact that Jonah had suffered writer's block for nearly three years – 1,070 days – and now merely taught creative writing at an obscure community college, might suggest that perhaps Jonah was not, in fact, a great writer on the verge of writing a great novel. However, whether the world demanded it or not, Jonah vowed that this next year would bring either noteworthy success or considerable change. He simply would not stand for another year of writer's block.

He had made the New Year's resolution a month early, writing and signing the ultimatum on a cocktail napkin at the bar. It was the kind of life-changing epiphany a drunken person has only when he's desperate – or a desperate person has only when he's drunk. Jonah now carried the folded cocktail napkin contract in his wallet. Only a week old, the resolution remained drastically important to Jonah. He would publish next year. He would write his First Great Novel. Things would change or his profession would change. However serious and committed, though, it appeared obvious that the inevitable writer's block breakthrough would not take place today.

Jonah blinked from his fixed stare on the window, took a final sip of his now-cold mug of whiskey and coffee, and exited the Microsoft Word program. As he did, an all-too-familiar and ever-so-annoying question appeared on the blank computer screen.

Save changes?

"If only there were something to change," Jonah mumbled to himself.

CHAPTER 3

*J*ONAH closed the laptop, grabbed his coat and left the apartment for his day job at the local community college. Despite the distance and the cold December chill, Jonah ignored the trolling taxis and opted to walk to work, as he always did, largely because of Miss Autumn Young.

Jonah made two routine stops during the fifteen-minute walk each morning on his way to enlighten college students on how to write, and do so creatively. First, he politely shook the hand of the old gentleman who owned The Downtown Newsstand, which, despite its name, was not located downtown. Jonah always bought the *New York Times* and *USA TODAY*. Jonah had no clue what the man's name was because, while they were never introduced nor did they ever exchange names, Jonah had been stopping at the newsstand every morning for more than two years, and it now seemed rude to ask his name. In addition, the owner had somehow learned Jonah's name, and was always good to greet him with a "Mornin', Jonah."

"Good morning, friend," Jonah would reply.

"A *New York Times* and *USA TODAY*, huh?"

"I suppose I am that predictable."

Jonah dropped a couple of dollars on the counter, folded both papers under his arm, and headed up the sidewalk.

"See you Monday, friend," Jonah said, leaving.

"Will do. Have a good one, Jonah."

With the news of the world in hand and the long, brown, leather strap of his worn briefcase swung over the opposite shoulder, Jonah quickened his pace toward his second regular morning stop. Soon he would engage in a sure-to-be delightful conversation with Autumn Young.

A 22-year-old senior at NYU, Autumn was eight years Jonah's junior. She had a slender body with all the curves that seem right for a young woman to have, a nice dark tan that Jonah thought drew even more attention to her legs, jet black hair like the color black seen when one closes one's eyes, and absolutely seductive amethyst-colored eyes. She was a young, beautiful co-ed with a smile worth waking up for. And, for about five minutes every morning, Autumn Young made Jonah feel young.

Jonah rounded another block and entered the closest of the city's three hundred twenty-three Starbucks locations. As always, the bell on the door announced the new customer, signaling several variations of "good morning" from the far-too-alert employees. Jonah exchanged the expected pleasantries as he made his way to his usual seat, a corner booth with its back against a window. Jonah put his briefcase down next to the table and set his newspapers on the tabletop. Autumn appeared from outside where she had just delivered two cappuccinos to a couple sitting on the covered porch. She innocently sat down across the table from Jonah.

"Good Morning, Mr. Frost," Autumn said in the cutest way possible.

"Miss Young," Jonah greeted.

"Isn't that the shirt you wore yesterday?" she asked.

"Yeah, I guess that I'm beyond the point of caring what I look like when I go to work. It's all I can do to show up anymore."

"Well, as long as you keep showing up *here*," Autumn responded, melting Jonah with a wink/smile combination. She reached for his hands, "let me see your palms."

Jonah willingly handed over his hands, delighted to have them holding something other than a bottle. Autumn turned them over and began tracing the lines of his palm with the smooth touch of her finger. Jonah's heart quickened.

"I'm no expert," she started, "but I do believe that I can read your near future."

"And what exactly is in store for me?" Jonah asked.

"Something you crave," she said, gently sliding her fingers across Jonah's hands. Her words came out slowly, building suspense.

"Go on."

"Something very sweet," Autumn said in an innocent voice.

"I like sweet."

"I see you tasting something extremely rich." With every word, Jonah leaned closer and closer to her, oblivious of the people around him.

"How soon do you think I'll be enjoying this rich pleasantry?" Jonah asked, his curiosity aroused.

"In about ten minutes," Autumn said, quickly letting go of Jonah's hands, abandoning her tempting act, and reverting to her normal voice and attitude. "I'll have your hot chocolate ready in no time so that you can appease your other addiction."

"Hot chocolate?" Jonah said in disappointment. He sat back in his booth. "Hey, what's my first addiction?" Jonah asked.

"Well, let me ask you, Mr. Frost. What's the other thing you come here for every single day?" Autumn gave another priceless wink and, though walking away, held Jonah's devoted attention even as she disappeared from his sight behind the counter.

Jonah picked up one of his papers and began to read the

headlines above the fold. Reading the news every morning was a habit Jonah's dad had instilled in him at an early age.

"Writers write so readers can read, but if you're going to write, you have to read," his dad was known to say.

So Jonah read. He read all the time, anything he could get his hands on. He read classic novels, biographies, history books, magazines, the latest bestseller, plays, poems, short stories, and prose. Anything from Salinger to Shakespeare, Golding to Grisham, Hemingway to Heraclitus, Fitzgerald to Far Side, Jonah read. And since his dad would customarily leave the morning paper on the kitchen table after reading it over breakfast, Jonah habitually read it as well.

"Getting some inspiration for your next book?" Autumn asked, eyeing his *New York Times* as she set a grande hot chocolate on the table.

"Not likely," Jonah said, snappier than he would have liked to. These days, he didn't enjoy any conversation about his writing.

"Well, whenever you do get inspired, you'd better let me read your book first, or at least name a character after me."

"How about you just let me take you out to dinner to celebrate once I finish it?" Jonah proposed.

"It's a date, Mr. Frost. I'll be praying that you find your story."

"Well, I've tried everything else. If you think praying will do the trick, then by all means, give it a shot."

"Jonah, we could all use a little prayer now and then." With one last wink, Autumn walked away.

Jonah took a sip of one of the few non-alcoholic drinks he still enjoyed, gathered his things, and incidentally sounded the bell once more as he opened the door to leave.

CHAPTER 4

As Abigail Jones examined the newborn baby lying on the desk in front of her, she scribbled notes of his symptoms and vital signs in a small notebook.

Yellow in whites of eyes. Fever. Vomiting. Dark-red urine.

The baby's crying persisted constantly and subsided only when Abigail gently scratched his stomach and arms. She added *Itching* to her list of symptoms. Jehené, the baby's mother, looked on, sharing in her son's pain, her wailing louder than that of the baby. A full two weeks had passed since she gave birth to Petpet, and he had yet to experience a day free from illness.

The grieving audience made Abigail nervous, causing her to yearn for her husband's return from the mountain. She always considered Memphis more qualified to treat patients. Surely he would be able to diagnose Petpet. Moreover, she hoped the hunters would hurry back so that Artone could comfort his wife. It was impossible for Abigail to concentrate in the midst of such crying and pressure.

Abigail handed the baby back to his mother and told her that Memphis would check on him again when he got back from hunting. Jehené's crying lessened as she took her baby and thanked Abigail. They both walked out of the hut, and Abigail watched as Jehené carried Petpet across the village and down the trail to their hut.

Abigail's general passion for the unsaved had gradually transformed into a bold, burning zeal for the Amarakaeri people of Duba. Jehené, along with a dozen other women of the village, had captured her heart years ago, leaving Abigail with an unmatched desire to see her friends fall in love with Christ. Now, with so many of them chasing after her Savior, she hoped to meet the physical needs that often accompanied the spiritual needs.

Around the Peruvian village, Abigail could see her friends and neighbors laboring over their early morning chores. A group of women carried children and pots down to the river to give baths and wash dishes, while a few other ladies squatted nearby as they blew hot coals to rekindle the fire for preparing breakfast.

Abigail distinctly heard the sound of metal scraping rock, the noise drowning out the chirping of the macaws flying past the tree line. Nearly every young man in the village sat busy sharpening his machete or fishing spear. Two elderly men quietly worked together to untangle a fishing net. Others headed out to their fields to gather leaves for roofs, logs for fire, or fruit for lunch.

Abigail felt the bottom of her shirt being tugged. She looked down and saw Cíba. Cíba boasted a birthmark on the left side of his face that resembled the shape of a jaguar's tooth. This unique distinction earned Cíba, even at the young age of five years old, a fair measure of popularity among his people.

"Katia'po?" Abigail asked. *What?*

With an invitation to speak, the little boy, who had apparently spent the first hours of the day playing in the muddy banks by the river, frantically began to tell a story. Since he had merely seen Memphis and Artone moments earlier, Cíba's report relied on his imagination rather than facts. Cíba ran around in circles gesticulating wildly as he acted out his tale. His words, mumbled and rushed, coupled with Abigail's difficulty in understanding the native dialect, failed to communicate much. She understood that he was trying to tell her something about Memphis and hunting, but even when Cíba acted like a man shooting arrows and throwing spears, Abigail remained completely lost.

"Menpihuej Budteré?" she asked, interrupting Cíba's charades act. *Where is Memphis?*

By this time, Cíba had reached the point of the story that required him to play the part of a jaguar. Upon hearing Abigail's question, he paused from crawling on all fours and pointed toward the forest. Out of the woods, stained in sweat-soaked blood and earth, Memphis walked down a barely-worn trail into the village. Draped over his shoulders like a fur coat, he wore the jaguar skin, still dripping blood from her mouth. Artone followed, dragging the meat of his trophy on a banana-leaf mat behind him.

A host of kids had already noticed the successful hunters and had joined them in their triumphant entrance. A few of the little ones proudly carried Memphis and Artone's weapons, while the rest jumped around with excitement and curiosity, asking for the story behind the jaguars. Neither Memphis nor Artone said a word, for they honored the tribe's custom of waiting until the entire village came together before they unveiled even the most insignificant detail. They would appropriately act out the story according to their culture that night over a fire. For now, they simply left the mystery to the imaginations of the children.

The hunting party reached Memphis and Abigail's hut where she stood staring at the blood running down Memphis's chest.

"Is that your blood?" she asked with a sense of worry and concern.

"No, that blood belongs to her," Memphis answered, dropping

the skin of the slain beast on the ground.

A few young men came, relieved Artone of his jaguar, and carried the meat to the community hut in the middle of the village. Artone squeezed Memphis's right bicep to praise him for a fine display of strength and placed his palm against Memphis's chest in order to recognize his impressive exhibition of courage. Memphis nodded and Artone turned to leave.

"Huamahueya, e'bape'kuhuit emin,'" Artone said as he walked toward the community hut. *We'll cook and eat this wild meat tonight.*

Abigail brushed some of the dirt off of Memphis's back and wiped away a spot of blood from his chin.

"You're filthy."

"Well, it's good to see you, too, beautiful," he said, leaning toward his wife.

Abigail smiled and gave Memphis a quick kiss.

"Your lips are dry."

"I don't think I've ever been more thirsty in my life," Memphis replied. "I'm starving, too."

"Come inside. I fried some bananas and filtered some water this morning."

Like the rest of the huts in the village, the construction of the Jones's hut primarily consisted of four strong logs about as thick as the fat end of a baseball bat. Since no Amarakaeri hut included walls, the logs had to be sturdy enough to bear the weight of the entire structure. The logs served as posts that supported the four corners of the roof, which consisted of giant banana leaves. The builders wove the stems of the leaves together on top of crisscrossed bamboo sticks, effectively protecting the interior of the hut from rain. The floor of the hut, though appearing thin as a leaf, was made up of narrowly cut capirona, and was elevated by a dozen short posts a foot and a half off the ground.

The single room was furnished with a large mosquito net covering a sleeping mat and sheet, a wooden table in one corner, three two-foot-tall tree trunks used as chairs, and two hammocks tied next to each other at the back of the hut. The structure featured no walls, no doors, no separate rooms, and no electricity. It was small and humble, and, according to the Joneses, it was "hut sweet hut."

"So are you going to tell me the story or do I have to wait like the others?"

Memphis was finishing his third banana and second liter of water. Abigail stood behind him, wiping his shoulders and back with a wet cloth.

"You can hear the whole thing tonight," he said. "But I will tell you that I've never been more scared. I truly thought I might die."

"You've thought that many times these past four years, haven't you?"

"This was different though, Babe. This was most definitely the closest call yet."

"Closer than the rockslide, or the jaguar, or the boat wreck, or the snake bite?"

"Yes. Much closer."

"Closer than the alligator?"

Memphis looked down and evaluated the three-inch-wide, six-inch-long scar on his left leg.

"Well, maybe it was as close as the alligator," he said.

"You worry me. I don't know how I could ever deal with

losing you. I mean I was even lonely just this morning when I woke up and you weren't lying next to me."

"I guess Art and I did leave pretty early last night. You shouldn't worry though. You know how the Lord protects us."

Memphis pulled Abigail into his lap. "Besides, I'm not going anywhere."

Memphis kissed Abigail who passionately kissed him back.

"Enough about me anyway," he said. "How was your morning? Any patients?"

"Petpet is sick again."

"What are his symptoms?"

"Fever, itching, vomiting, yellow in his eyes."

"Did you get a urine sample?"

"Dark red."

"Diarrhea?"

"No."

"So what do you think?"

"I don't know. Hepatitis or malaria. Could be a severe case of malaria; especially if the yellow in his eyes is jaundice."

"You said he's itching, right?"

"Right."

"I'll check on him this afternoon. How's Jenny?"

"Borderline hysterical. She cried the entire time I was examining Petpet."

"She'll be better now that Art is back."

Abigail nodded in agreement and leaned her head against Memphis's chest ignoring the sweat, dirt, and blood. Memphis continued to hold her in his arms as he silently prayed for the healing of his best friend's son.

"Hey," Abigail said, raising her head. "Speaking of Art, what did he say when he was walking off? Something about cooking?"

"He said they're going to cook the jaguar meat tonight. I guess it'll be part of our going away party."

Reminiscent of the first night of their honeymoon, Memphis stood and carried Abigail over the threshold and out of their hut. Not wanting to show too much affection nor draw a great deal of attention, Abigail jumped out of Memphis's arms and walked beside him as they trekked through the Amazon jungle to their favorite spot in the indigenous village of Duba.

The fifteen-foot waterfall and the small, freshwater pool that it creates are hidden by a fortress of spear-like trees whose leaves form an isolating canopy and serve as the perfect escape for the young missionaries. Memphis threw his shorts aside and dived into the cool water. Allowing the waterfall to run over his head, he leaned back and scrubbed the dirt and blood off his chest and stomach.

Coming out of the fall, Memphis froze when he noticed Abigail standing on the shore. Memphis didn't blink once. She had tan, smooth skin, and a body that didn't appear to have aged one minute since the day they first met. She waded into the waters, dived under the surface, and came up in Memphis's arms, her chest against his.

"Can you believe we're leaving this place?" Abigail asked.

Memphis looked around at the beauty of the hidden paradise they had affectionately come to call Our Spot. Clear water poured over into the circular pool like a heavy rain rolling off the edge of a leaf roof. An array of parrots frequented the trees above as florescent blue butterflies covered the grass on the ground. Flowers and berries and fruits grew abundantly, and it was the one place in the jungle not dominated by mosquitoes and flies. Aside from the occasional visiting monkey, the quiet area guaranteed privacy.

"It is sort of surreal that we're leaving tomorrow," Memphis said. "God has given us so many memories here at Our Spot."

Abigail pulled him closer.

"I think we have time for one more," she said.

As the sun reached its peak of the day, in the cool waters below, Memphis drank in the love of his young bride to the familiar and pleasant sound of their waterfall.

After checking on Petpet, leaving Promethazine pills for the vomiting and Chloroquine to treat malaria, Memphis spent the rest of the afternoon skinning the jaguar and eating papaya with Artone as they lay in hammocks, talking in the community hut. Abigail boiled a plate-full of yucca for Jehené, who stayed in her mosquito net with Petpet all day.

As Memphis and Artone finished their papaya, Abigail sat on the floor talking with Jehené, and Petpet slept peacefully for the first time in days. The descending sun colored the sky with light purple streaks that beautifully invaded and interlaced with the bleeding horizon stretching beyond Duba, reaching toward the unknown and forgotten. The quiet, still, and practically empty village began to awake with life as the men and women returned from their fields.

Most of the men journeyed down to the river for a quick bath before the evening festivities. Women busied themselves hauling pots and rice and bananas and yucca and baskets of other fruits and vegetables to the clay stove in the community hut. The older men began to paint their faces and decorate themselves with colorful feathers. Alone in his hut, the chief

put on the traditional dress, face paint, feather, and his crown. Artone and Memphis parted as they walked to their respective huts where they and their wives prepared for the party.

CHAPTER 5

WHATEVER amount of joy and satisfaction Jonah's conversation with Autumn may have brought to the cold December morning just as quickly disappeared when he arrived at his office. Suddenly Jonah felt very much like the weather: cold and damp.

Had it not been the end of the semester, the note on Jonah's office door would not have worried him in the least. For the dean of the English Department to desire a meeting with Jonah now though, could only mean one thing, namely, another demand for Jonah to publish. He put the note from the dean in his pocket, remembering the folded napkin contract in his back pocket, and entered his office.

Jonah had taught at the city's smallest community college for two and a half years, and, while boasting one of the youngest tenures, was granted a decent-size office with a generous view of a beautiful courtyard and garden located in the middle of the campus. This was partly due to the fortunate coincidence that the office had recently become vacated and thus available weeks before the dean hired Jonah. Jonah's previous two years of experience as an NYU creative writing professor made him a reasonable candidate for the prime space. However, the most likely reason that Jonah uncharacteristically received a large office upon arrival found its root in the legend of his father. Unfortunately, other faculty resented this undeserved preferential treatment, and it proved difficult for Jonah to make friends among his peers.

On the walls of Jonah's arguably undeserved office were various framed awards, his college degree, and a few black-and-white photos of beautiful places around the world where he had never been. His brother had given him a fancy wooden nameplate with gold lettering trimmed finely in black that now sat near the front edge of Jonah's desk. An unorganized mess of books, stories to grade, writing journals, magazines, a few files, and some old newspapers lay on his desk. It was the traditional desktop scene generally seen in offices of people who work hard and often late. In Jonah's case, however, the clutter merely reflected his messiness, laziness, and apathy.

Against one wall stood a six-shelf bookcase, while another four-shelf unit adorned the adjoining wall. Both bookcases were completely full of books that Jonah did not write. At least that's how Jonah saw it lately. He kept a scarf and coat rack in the corner on one side of the door, and an antique globe from his parents on the other side. All decorating had taken place within the first three hours of his first day. Since then, Jonah had neither added to nor rearranged anything in his office except the constantly shifting and growing pile on his desk.

He did find time, though, to frequently spin and study the globe during afternoons that should have been occupied with grading or writing. He knew geography well, though he had yet to leave the country. Jonah always included the "yet," for he had big traveling plans once he finished his novel. Like everything else in his life, though, he kept those plans on hold until the day his book hit the market.

Jonah dug the note from the dean out of his pocket and sat down behind his desk. After reading it two more times, Jonah opened the bottom left drawer to grab an unwashed glass and the half-empty bottle of bourbon (nothing in Jonah's life was considered to be half-full). He was due in class in ten minutes but could not care less. Besides, the students would wait. They always did.

Jonah set the glass on the dean's note. He read the note again, through the bottom of the glass, then filled the glass with bourbon. His throat used to burn when he drank hard liquor, but since his divorce Jonah had spent countless days growing accustomed to the taste. He finished the glass and poured another. Then another. He was now ten minutes late for his last class of the semester.

I don't care if it's the last class I teach for the rest of my life, Jonah thought.

He reluctantly took a few books and folders out of his briefcase, put a couple of different ones into his briefcase, unpleasantly dwelled once more on the dean's note and the rapidly-approaching dreaded meeting, and then headed to class. The instant he entered the room, he regretted leaving the bourbon behind.

"Did you get a chance to read my story yet, Mr. Frost?"

Although Jonah had his back turned to the student while he arranged a few things on his desk, the voice was unmistakably recognizable.

"Not yet, Mitch," Jonah answered without turning around and in a tone that clearly meant to end the unsolicited conversation.

Mitch nodded and took his seat. Jonah couldn't help but think of how irritating the persistent student was, always writing and seeking even a hint of approval or encouragement. Jonah found it all quite infuriating. The truth was Mitch had talent and reminded Jonah a bit of himself in the not-too-distant past. And that annoyance resided deep within the community college professor.

Although the syllabus indicated that the day's lecture would speak to the relation between a good story and good writing, Jonah rarely followed, or was even aware of, the syllabus. He had planned to pass the hour work-shopping short stories the students had turned in the previous week. However, after Mitch asked some tiresome question about the lecture on the syllabus, Jonah, frustrated and extremely apathetic, changed his mind.

"We're not going to have that lecture today, Mitch," he said. "In fact, we're not going to do anything. I have a meeting with the dean. Class is canceled today."

"But this is our last class of the semester," Mitch protested.

"Well then, Mitch, class is canceled for the semester. Have a good holiday, everybody."

Jonah lazily lifted his briefcase from the desk, looked over the dazed students staring at their hung-over professor, and then walked out of the room in search of another drink.

CHAPTER 6

BACK in his office, Jonah finished his bottle of bourbon and then fell asleep at his desk for half an hour. When he woke up and raised his head from the desk, the dean's note was stuck to the side of his face. He peeled off the note, crumpled it up, and tossed it into his wastebasket. In a drunken slur, Jonah began to curse the dean, the entire English Department, and his ex-wife.

Clumsily, he knocked the receiver of the phone off its base. Jonah slowly, and with great difficulty due to his malfunctioning motor skills, foolishly dialed a memorized phone number from the past.

"NYU English Department; how may I direct your call?"

"Extension 187, please," Jonah managed to say in a tone that made the secretary assume he was either drunk or ill with a swollen tongue.

"One moment please," the secretary said.

Jonah dipped his finger in the empty glass on his desk, soaking up the last few drops of liquor. He rubbed his finger over his tongue, absorbing what little bourbon he could.

"This is Professor Paige Johnson," a voice answered.

Jonah hated hearing her maiden name.

"Well good morning, Professor Paige," Jonah mumbled. "And how is the NYU English Department?"

"Jonah? Is that you?" Jonah could picture her rolling her eyes. "Have you been drinking again?" she asked.

"I may have little boozed. I mean, boozed a little. But I am *not* drunk." Jonah burped and could taste a bit of vomit that he promptly swallowed. "I was just thinking about you."

"I can't do this right now. I have a class in less than an hour."

"I canceled my class. You should just cancel your class, because then…you know what, Paige? Then, you wouldn't have to go to class."

"That's quite profound of you, Jonah, but I think I'll show up anyway just to see if I can maybe teach a thing or two."

"Oh, I bet you can. You're a great teacher. No, not great, brilliant. You are the most brillantest teacher I've ever saw."

"Thank you, Jonah. You were a great teacher once, too."

"But not a great husband."

"Don't do this to yourself, Jonah."

"Why did you leave me, Paige? I loved you. Why did you stop loving me?" There was a whimper in his voice, a hint of crying. He banged his head once on his desk and left it there as Paige responded.

"Jonah, we have been through this a million times. You know I loved you. It's just that we worked together all day long and when we got home, all we talked about was work – the same old stuff about the students and the faculty – and the books you intended to write. That's if we talked at all. But most of the time, you just sat in front of your computer for hours, writing."

"I'm a writer, Paige!" Jonah shouted into the phone as he jerked his head up from the desk. "That's what writers do. They write! Write! Write! Write!" Jonah's infuriated yelling escalated until his throat burned from the strain.

Baited, Paige retaliated.

"And when, exactly, was the last time you – Jonah the writer – wrote anything?" she sarcastically asked, raising her voice considerably. "I'm not just talking about being published. I know you haven't done that in years. I'm asking, when was the last time you even wrote anything? Anything, Jonah?"

"What would you know about it, Paige?"

"I know you're a washed-up, lonely drunk with incurable writer's block."

Jonah stood up from his desk in preparation for his quick, witty, highly insulting comeback. Nothing of that description came to mind. He instead resorted to a playground defense.

"You know your last name sounds stupid, Paige *Johnson*," Jonah said. "I liked you better when you were Paige Frost." And with that, he slammed the phone down and fell back into his chair, covering his face with his shaking hands.

Exhausted from the unpleasant phone call, Jonah fell asleep again at his desk. Two hours later, Jonah awoke in a disoriented haze, confused by his surroundings. He emptied a bottle of Advil onto his desk, and picked up two pills that he tossed into his mouth, swallowing them without the aid of water. He peered into his wastebasket where he was reminded of the dean's note. Antagonized by the sheer thought of the dean's obtuse, presumptuous, interfering agenda, Jonah kicked the wastebasket like a soccer ball, and stormed out of his office. After zigzagging down the hallway, he threw open the double glass doors at the end of the hall.

"I'm sorry sir, you can't just go in there; you must have an appointment." The dean's secretary, previously distracted by her one hundredth game of solitaire, had not noticed Jonah until his hand was already on the doorknob of the dean's office.

Jonah paused, turned around, and slammed the wadded note down on the secretary's desk.

"I have an appointment," Jonah snapped.

Self-authorized, Jonah barged into the dean's office.

The dean of the English Department, Dr. Richard White, had held the title for more than ten years. He was a white-haired, overweight, bitter man who would take a red pen and have an editing frenzy with works of William Faulkner and Charles Dickens if he could. Although Dr. White had never published any fiction of his own, he was quick to point out the publishing failures and writing downfalls of all he encountered. Jonah loathed the dean's unwarranted arrogance.

Dr. White was in the middle of a phone call when Jonah burst in.

"You wanted to see me?" Jonah said with surprisingly clear diction. Thanks to his nap, Jonah had recovered from his swollen-tongue and drunken slur.

"Why don't you have a seat outside, Professor Frost?" Dr. White said, covering the mouthpiece of the phone with his hand. "I'll be with you momentarily."

"Did you or did you not leave me a note saying that you wanted to see me?" Jonah purposefully asked loudly enough to be heard by whatever pompous jerk was on the other end of the line.

"I'll have to call you back, Gene," Dr. White said before hanging up the phone. Impatiently, he looked up at Jonah. "Why don't you have a seat, Professor Frost?" It was a direction more than a query.

"I'll stand. I'm in a hurry. So what do you want?"

"Jonah, I think you know why we're meeting today."

"Publishing requirements?"

"That's correct. The English Department requires all full-time professors to publish each semester. Now, although your previous accomplishments are undoubtedly impressive and noteworthy, you have failed to produce any published work during your four semesters of teaching here."

Jonah found Dr. White's tone absolutely condescending. Furthermore, Jonah thought it hilarious that a small New York City community college struggling to bring in enough tuition to pay the electric bill masqueraded as a real institution of higher learning by holding its professors to the same standards as a large state university.

"Jonah, while it pains me to say this, I'm afraid that you are not going to be able to teach here next semester," Dr. White said. "Two years without publishing a word is just too long."

"It's actually been three years," Jonah said with more than just a hint of sarcasm.

"What?" Dr. White asked.

"You said that I hadn't published anything in two years. It's really been closer to three years since I've been published; 1,070 days to be exact."

"Oh. Right. Well, maybe this is what you need then, a break so that you can concentrate on your writing."

Jonah rolled his eyes and began to walk around the office, examining the books and pictures decorating shelves and walls. Dr. White continued to lecture.

"I know that people expect much of you, Jonah, and I understand that the pressure to publish can be overwhelming; but you must see that in this profession, two years is an awfully long time."

Dr. White's words were like an onslaught of arrows that only served to arouse the anger of the wounded giant. And the dean's quiver was about to be emptied with one final blow.

"In the end, Jonah, your writer's block or complacency or depression or laziness or apathy or, perhaps, your failed marriage, or whatever it is that has kept you from meeting the college's publishing requirements these past few years has become a grave disappointment to the entire department. While unfortunate, I do hope that this termination will give you the long overdue wake-up call that we writers sometimes need."

A boiling rage stirred deep within Jonah's soul like a pit of fiery red lava inside the belly of a dormant volcano. With words like "laziness," "publishing requirements," "failed marriage," "grave disappointment," "termination," and "long overdue," the hot lava began to rise and threaten an awakening. When the dean said, "we writers," as if the fat, unpublished, balding dean was worthy to be compared with the talented Jonah Frost, as though Dr. White was any kind of writer at all, the volcano erupted.

"You don't have a clue what you're talking about!" Jonah shouted. "You, a writer? You're not fit to scribble a grocery list. If I settled for worthless trash that would be better suited for toilet paper than literature like all the other hacks of this laughable department, then I could be published tomorrow. True talent, though, demands a higher standard, and can't be conjured up at any given moment by your ridiculous publishing requirements. Apathy? Laziness? Writer's block? My divorce? No, Richard, I'm unable to write because I'm surrounded by mediocrity and the celebration of average work.

"You do me a favor to free me from this dead-end cliché so that I might remember the levels of excellence that used to surround me. I will finish my novel, and you'll be begging me to come back here and sign your copy."

Jonah neared the desk, and Dr. White stood so that the two enraged men were nose to nose.

"You're a has-been, Jonah," Dr. White shot back, fuming. "You stopped writing before you came here, and you're not going to be able to write after you leave. You're done. You're *not* a writer. You're *not* a teacher. What you *are* is washed-up and fired. Now get out of my office!"

"I'm washed-up? Look at you. I don't know how you kid yourself every day into thinking that you actually contribute something to this school. You come in, sit at your desk, fire and complain and criticize, and then you go home and brag about your wonderful position as dean. You're worthless. At least I'm trying to write, trying to teach, trying to do something."

"You're not trying to teach. You show up for work late and hung-over and by the time you go home, you're drunk again. You shamelessly sport dirty clothes, sloppy hair, unshaved scruff, and an altogether, unkempt appearance. You are careless, disorganized, and apathetic. If your father hadn't been someone, you would have been fired a year ago. Now get out!"

Jonah flipped two chairs over, knocked an autographed picture of Lou Gehrig off the wall, and violently slammed the door on his way out. The secretary awkwardly attempted to occupy herself with another game of solitaire as Jonah passed by, retrieving the dean's note from her desk.

Jonah concluded it would be best to clean out his office on Saturday when the dean would most assuredly be home adding pounds and ripping on brilliant writers. Slamming another door as he walked outside, Jonah threw the dean's note on the ground and grumbled something about how it should have been pink.

CHAPTER 7

*T*HE chanting could be heard as far as the smoke could be seen. As they finished devouring the remaining scraps of fried jaguar meat, all fourteen families of the tribal Amarakaeri village, Duba, crowded around the enormous bonfire blazing just outside the community hut. The celebrative dances had begun.

Every native arrived adorned in festive tribal dress, garments made from strips of rough bark ripped from the plentiful capirona trees that surrounded the Peruvian village. Beaten into thin sheets of material and sown together, the dried bark became a durable fabric. Their outfits were decorated with coal markings and enhanced with a fringe of feathers around the bottom.

Each indigenous man bore a thin wooden peg pierced through his nose with small blue or green feathers sticking out from either end. Even the youngest man proudly boasted necklaces made of assorted bones and teeth from various hunting triumphs, while several of the older men boasted branded forearms revealing numerous spear tattoos, each representing an enemy kill in battle. The chief alone sported a long rope-braided necklace that hung down to his naval, where a sharp, wooden arrowhead was attached. All tribal members recognized the chief as the strongest, bravest warrior.

The males squatted on the ground in a semi-circle, facing Memphis and Abigail whom they honored with the head seats. Even the chief forfeited his right to sit at the center of attention, joining the rest of the men in the chanting and percussion that accompanied the dancing of the women. The men held thick, green, hollow bamboo sticks, cut at different lengths, which produced a harmony of melodious tones when the chanting men bounced them rhythmically against the ground. The music echoed through the star-painted night on beat with the sound of a dozen bare feet pounding the hard ground.

Encircled by the men, the native women moved about in a synchronized, yet somewhat syncopated fashion. At times, the group tirelessly leapt up and down behind a soloist who would slowly sway toward Memphis and Abigail while swinging her hips and shaking her outspread arms in the motion of ocean waves. Suddenly, she would rejoin the dancers just in time for the throng to divide into three groups, each displaying a distinct routine of its own. The bamboo percussion, chanting, and dancing continued for more than two hours. Memphis and Abigail enjoyed the show, taking to heart every last moment of this beautiful expression of an ancient culture and glorious reflection of such a rich heritage.

When the dancing, at last, came to an end, the chief stood at Memphis's side and the exhausted women filled the open spaces in the semi-circle as Artone piled another stack of logs onto the fire.

"Remember Memphis, I want you to translate everything," Abigail said. "I don't want to miss a single word tonight."

With his hand on Memphis's shoulder, the chief began to address the crowd. Memphis quietly translated for his wife who leaned in closely to listen.

"Tonight, we honor two friends, born of a different tribe."

Memphis paused to hear the next part. With every carefully chosen word of his well-versed speech, the chief spoke with poise and dignity in front of his admiring, captivated audience. Memphis barely whispered as he related the discourse.

"Not too many moons have passed since we encountered these, our first strangers. Yet much has changed in such a short time. For no longer do we call them strangers nor treat them as outsiders, rather we count them as friends, kin of our people. With us, they have known sickness and good health, hunger and plenty, mourning and laughter. With us, they have lived. With us, they have shared their lives, as our lives have been shared with them.

"Many of you have come to know the Jesus that they speak of, and this new faith has changed you. The rest of us see that this has proven to be a good change. In fact, I believe that all of our memories with Budteré and Abby, save one, are indeed good ones. Let us now remember the day that began our journey with our white neighbors. Artone and Jehené have volunteered to help us reenact the first day that we met Budteré and Abby."

The Amarakaeri people of Duba regard story telling as the highest form of communication and entertainment. Any story worth telling must be told properly, with emotion, dramatics, and an audience. The best storytellers remain among the most highly respected members of the village. However, even though Artone and Jehené rarely storied, the rest of the community yielded the privilege to the closest friends of the missionaries.

"They're not really going to act out the rockslide, are they?" Abigail asked.

"That's what the chief said," Memphis answered.

"How embarrassing!"

Artone and Jehené moved to the center of the circle. Four

young men and the chief grabbed spears and stood in front of them.

"I think that Art and Jenny are playing the parts of you and me," Memphis whispered to Abigail.

"Oh, this is going to be hilarious. Jenny said that she had a surprise for me."

Just before the theatrics commenced, Artone remembered his costume and ran out of the circle and behind a tree. When he rejoined the group, he wore a long blond wig made of bright yellow Macaw feathers. Immediately, the entire village became a soundtrack of laughter. Memphis's long blond hair had long been a novelty in Duba, drawing curiosity and even earning Memphis the nickname Budteré, the name of a jungle worm with fluffy blond hair that stings whoever dares to touch it.

"I guess you were right," Abigail said. "Art is definitely playing you."

The skit began as Artone and Jehené walked up to the other men and waved as if greeting them for the first time. The men poked Artone in the chest with their spears and began to scream angrily in his direction. Suddenly they stopped yelling when they noticed Jehené. Two of the men walked over to her and started playing with her hair. Pointing at Abigail, the crowd laughed, and some of the kids, in a moment of improvisation, ran over to her and grabbed and tangled Abigail's hair, mimicking the on-going comedy in the middle of the circle.

Taking their cue, three of the women jumped from their spots and shook their fingers at the men admiring Jehené's hair. One of the women accidentally broke character when a slight gust of wind tossed Artone's wig onto the ground. With her uncontrollable outbursts of laughter, the actress sent everyone, including the rest of the cast, into fits of hysterical laughter that only increased when Artone casually and unevenly put the wig back on top of his head.

Once the actors regained their composure, they huddled around the chief, excluding Artone and Jehené. With authority, the chief issued an order and the men broke from the circle and took hold of Artone and Jehené. Leading them with spears in their backs, the men ushered them around the circle as the women and the chief followed, simulating the long walk on which they originally led Memphis and Abigail. After a few laps, the chief took hold of Artone's arm and led him outside the circle. The crowd grew quiet. Tension weighed heavily on the silence. With remorse, everyone in the village remembered what they had intended to do next. No one looked forward to reliving the regretful, unpleasant memory.

"It's hard to imagine that people who are now like family to us, truly planned to kill us," Memphis said to Abigail.

"I still get chills when I think about this part," Abigail said. "I remember standing there crying with spears all around me, just praying that the Lord would rescue you."

"And He did."

Still tightly gripping Artone's arm, the chief tiptoed a couple of steps further. He carefully studied the ground, acting like he was looking out over a steep cliff. Turning to yell something to the group that surrounded Jehené with weapons, the chief raised his long spear, and turned back towards Artone, ready to push him over the imaginary cliff. Stepping into their roles, the rest of the village began drumming their hands forcefully against the ground. The chief looked up behind him to see what caused the thunder.

"E'tihuarak huid! E'tihuarak huid!" one of the men shouted.
"Rock slide! Rock slide!" Memphis repeated the call to Abby.

The men and women standing in the circle ran with Jehené away from the implied, thundering mountain. Artone picked up the chief and dove backwards just as a host of kids threw rocks at the spot where they previously stood. The chief stood up with Artone and slowly walked back into the circle. The rest of the cast joined him with Jehené, the men still pointing their spears at the "foreigners." The chief looked over all the faces of the village and nodded. The men dropped their spears and immediately the audience erupted with loud shouts of approval and applause.

CHAPTER 8

*F*OLLOWING the rehearsed reenactment, Memphis and Artone's impromptu mini-drama seemed quite amateur. Nevertheless, as the two hunters employed the basic props of bows, arrows, and spears to finally unveil the long awaited tale of the two jaguar kills, the crowd showed no signs of discontent. Cíba, the boy with the birthmark, managed to cast himself to play the part of both jaguars. The men jeered Artone when his arrow and spear missed, and everyone laughed as Cíba dramatically died with an arrow stuck under his armpit giving the appearance that it had pierced through his body. Abigail nearly fainted when Memphis slid onto the ground to grab Artone's spear a split second before the female jaguar reached him. Abundant laughter ensued when Artone finally realized that he was still wearing the blond wig from the previous skit.

Out of breath, Memphis sat back down next to Abigail who continued laughing with the rest of the village.

"Well, I wouldn't award you an Oscar or anything, but I don't suppose it was that bad," Abigail joked.

"Hey, I'd like to see you slide into the dirt while some jungle kid is jumping all over you."

"You'd really like to see that?" Abigail asked, laughing.

Memphis smiled. "You know what I mean," he said.

Silencing the rest of the group, Artone placed himself between Memphis and Abigail to make an announcement. Memphis quietly translated for Abigail.

"He said that they have a tradition here in Duba, that whenever someone travels outside the village, the rest of the community sends them off into the river."

"Sends them into the river?" Abigail questioned. "What in the world does that mean?"

Her question still hanging in the air, a dozen women unexpectedly lifted Abigail from her seat. Simultaneously, Artone led a group of men to hoist Memphis into the air, lifting him as high as possible with their out-stretched arms. As the entire village followed, sounding tribal chants along the way, the men and women holding Memphis and Abigail above their heads carried them down a trail to the shadowy riverbanks.

Artone signaled the two groups, and without further warning, the men and women tossed Memphis and Abigail into the cold waters of the calm river. All by-standers were splattered by the splash. Covered in goose bumps, with chills and chattering teeth, the soaked missionaries burst out of the water for air.

Laughing, Memphis whispered something to Abigail. They

both swam to the bank where Artone and Jehené reached down to help them out of the river. Memphis and Abigail took their hands and then pulled their native friends into the chilly waters. As soon as Artone's head broke the surface, Memphis jumped up, put his hands on top of Artone's wet hair and, to the expressed approval of the rest of the village, dunked him under the water again.

Artone playfully retaliated, and while the men wrestled one another in the splashing waters, Abigail and Jehené raced each other to a shallow spot where they stood to get out of the river. Just when they had settled their first step onto the bank, Memphis and Artone surprised them from behind, effortlessly picked them up, and fell backwards into the water still holding their wives. A moment later, with the women sitting on the men's shoulders, the four engaged in a familiar game the two families had often enjoyed playing ever since the Joneses first taught Artone and Jehené how to "chicken fight." As quickly as it had begun, however, the match was interrupted.

Without drawing any attention to himself, the chief had quietly slipped away from the raucous crowd about the time Memphis dunked Artone under the water. He went up the hill to the village, past the community hut, then veered toward the direction of the river, and disappeared into a small huddle of trees that overlooked the crowded banks. There, the chief, without rustling the branches, or making any sound at all for that matter, untangled a long rope firmly tied to the strongest branch of the tree.

Just as the spectators began to make predictions as to who would win the chicken fight, the chief shouted from the top of the hill, "Budteré!" Quite unceremoniously, he then swung out beyond the banks and over the river where he let go of the rope and crashed into the water. Every mouth in Duba hung wide open. Abigail dismounted, dropping off Memphis's shoulders. Seconds went by and the chief had yet to resurface. While the village waited, the chief swam underwater and surfaced directly behind Memphis.

"Budteré!" he shouted again.

Before Memphis could turn around, the chief wrapped his arms around Memphis and pulled him under the water. Laughter filled the air once more, streaming out from the lively banks. As Memphis wildly shook his long hair like a dog with wet fur, a host of men, women and children alike jumped into the disturbed river with loud hollers and shouts that seemed to reach the stars. The few women who stayed behind on the dry banks reassumed their dancing roles, while the men who resisted the temptation of following the crowd into the river gathered their bamboo sticks and accompanied the native dances with upbeat percussion sounds.

In the river, the community tossed kids, skipped rocks, dunked one another, and held chicken fight tournaments. Smoke from the bonfire lifted into the night with the chants, music, and laughter, as the villagers played, swam, and danced, wishing a good journey to their foreign friends; and all to the glorious backdrop of sparkling constellations, shooting stars, and a full moon that served to just barely highlight the dense jungle tree line.

CHAPTER 9

*A*LONE in his apartment, Jonah spent the afternoon replaying the conversations he had had with Paige and the dean. Every now and then, he would actually feel optimistic about his unsolicited holiday. One minute would find him cursing the pretentious dean, and the next completely relaxed on his couch as he found comfort in the possibility that this surprising turn of events could be the breakthrough he had long needed. Perhaps a semester off would allow him to devote the time his First Great Novel deserved. A moment later, however, the thought would fade, and Jonah would curse the dean again.

He extinguished the sulking for good when he, at last, grabbed a book from the coffee table and, reclining on his couch, began to read. Before the end of the first chapter, Jonah fell asleep to dream of better years.

Jonah's older brother, Noah Frost, was a distinguished linguist at the New York Institute of Languages and was well respected by his colleagues. He had long been Jonah's lone faithful supporter and was the only other person in the world who quite expected that his little brother would most certainly, one day, write an excellent novel.

Noah and Jonah had been close while growing up, had re-attached when Noah moved back to the city after their parents died, and ever since both brothers' divorces, had been inseparable. Every Friday night found Noah and Jonah meeting together at their favorite Italian restaurant to catch up on anything significant from the week, and more important, to distract themselves from the depressing truth that they were both lonely and dateless on a Friday night. This primary reason behind the dinner was never mentioned, though mutually accepted.

When Jonah woke up from his unintended nap, he had but thirty minutes to shower, dress, and meet Noah for their standing eight o'clock reservation. Jonah felt no need to rush because he knew his brother would arrive on time to claim the table.

When Jonah did finally arrive, the maitre d' showed him to their usual table for two. Noah sat waiting, pouring his first glass of white wine.

"I hope you can find a designated driver for this drunk at the end of the night," Jonah joked to the maitre d', both of them eyeing Noah. Professionally, the maitre d' simply nodded and returned to the front of the restaurant.

Typically, Noah only drank one glass of wine with his dinner, but after waiting for Jonah for forty-five minutes, he had decided to have a drink.

"Didn't I give you a watch for Christmas last year?" Noah asked as Jonah took his seat.

"I fell asleep. Sorry."

"Did you fall asleep or pass out?"

"Don't start with all of that, Noah. Can't I just enjoy a nice dinner with my big brother?"

"I'm sorry. You're right. It's just that your eyes are very red. Did you have a bad day?"

"The worst," Jonah said, filling his glass with wine.

"What happened? You didn't call Paige again, did you?"

"No. It was a bad day at work."

"Oh."

"I mean, yes, I did call Paige and, yes, that was horrible as always, but that's not what made my day miserable. Dr. White, the dean, took care of that."

Before Jonah could elaborate, a waiter appeared with a host of information about the evening's many specials. Jonah always thought it absurd to have so many specials. How can half the menu be special, he wondered silently, and what does that say about the rest of the menu? While the waiter rattled off his memorized speech, Jonah drank his wine and looked around the room.

The preferred Italian restaurant of the Frost brothers was an eloquent little place downtown called House of Rome. Every man – or "gentleman," as the maitre d' referred to all male customers – wore a nice and usually expensive suit, complemented by a tie and a shave. And every lady displayed an elegant dress with the finest jewelry to match. At the House of Rome, even average looking women and men appeared beautiful and handsome. All carried themselves in the most polite and respectable manner. The House of Rome was a place where important people went to enjoy their prestige and rich people went to prove their wealth.

For Noah and Jonah it was simply a place where they were still recognized as their father's sons. This propriety was enough to secure the brothers a weekly reservation at the prestigious House of Rome. Noah nearly always fronted the bill.

After ordering, Noah slowly sipped his wine as Jonah finished his first glass and poured himself another. A second waiter brought their salads the moment the first waiter left with their entrée order. Jonah had a mouthful of crouton and lettuce when Noah finished biding his time.

"I assume there's more to the story," Noah probed.

"The story is that there is no story," Jonah said, half swallowing and half chewing.

"No story? Wait, don't tell me that the dean is on your case again about publishing requirements."

"That's exactly what it was."

"Doesn't he understand that it takes time, finesse, to write a book?"

"He wouldn't know a good book if I hit him in the head with it; even if I hit him in the head over and over and over...."

"I get the picture, Jonah. So, what do you have to do? Write a few short stories real quick, get published, and get the dean off your back?"

"Noah, I was fired today."

"What? Just like that? No warning?"

"He said that two years without publishing anything was just too long." Jonah took another bite of his salad and two more sips of wine.

"Can't you just publish and get your job back so that you'll have something to do next semester while you finish your novel?" Noah asked.

Jonah appreciated how Noah always said that Jonah was "finishing" his novel, implying that he had already started writing it. They both knew this to be untrue, but it was a harmless lie that encouraged Jonah nonetheless.

"Well, I really don't think that Dr. White would hire me back even if I won the Pulitzer Prize tomorrow."

"Why? What did you say?"

"I said a lot, Noah. He was arrogant and insulting, and I let him know how I felt."

"And how, exactly, do you feel?"

"I feel that someone who can't write or publish doesn't have the right to demand it from someone else. I also told him that he shouldn't call me lazy and careless and disorganized and drunk, and he shouldn't talk about my ex-wife."

"He mentioned Paige?"

"One of his theories as to why I haven't published lately is that I'm depressed about my divorce."

"That was years ago," Noah said, defending his brother.

"Yeah, years ago. It was also years ago that I published anything," Jonah said quietly. He finished his second glass of wine.

"Why don't you slow down on that?" Noah suggested as Jonah filled another glass.

"I'll save this one for dinner," Jonah conceded.

Yet another waiter that Noah and Jonah had not seen before came and cleared their empty plates, while a fourth waiter followed to wipe the table clean. A waitress brought a new set of clean silverware, and the young man who took their order returned with their dinner.

"So what's been going on with you?" Jonah asked. Both were cutting into their steaming dinner.

"Well, I did receive some big news today," Noah said.

"A raise? A promotion?"

"Not exactly. My boss has selected me to lead the initial research phase of a native language study."

Like the rest of the family, Noah was in love with words. Unlike his father and brother, however, this infatuation had not led him to write, but rather, to translate. Foreign languages fascinated him and he had the job to prove it.

"So what language is it?" Jonah asked. "What country speaks it?"

"It's an indigenous language spoken only in Peru. Apparently, there's a tribe in the jungles there that was only recently located. There are only about ninety of them in the whole world."

"That sounds different," Jonah said. "How, though, are you supposed to study some language of a small group of jungle men way out there in Peru?"

"I'm scheduled to depart the day after Christmas and return to New York for debriefing the first of April."

"The day after Christmas? That's in two weeks, Noah. You've already planned all of this? Shouldn't we have talk about it first?"

"I know it's short notice, Jonah."

Jonah poked at his pasta, considering the idea of Noah being gone for three months.

"It's a wonderful opportunity and a pretty big step for me at the language institute," Noah added.

"Well, that it is, big brother," Jonah agreed. He raised his fourth glass of wine. "A toast to Noah Frost, the most brilliant linguist in the Amazon jungle. Cheers!"

Noah touched his glass to Jonah's and took another sip of his first glass of wine.

"Thank you, Jonah," Noah said.

"So what will you be doing in the jungle?" Jonah asked. "Are you going to live in huts and swim with anacondas and all of that?"

"I don't really know what to expect. My assignment is to conduct a preliminary study on the dialect spoken there and to determine if there are any relationships to other languages previously discovered in that area."

"Sounds like an adventure. Difficult, but adventurous. And you're really going to be gone for three months?"

"That's right. Hey, why don't you come with me?" Noah asked.

"Come with you to the jungle?"

"Sure. I could say you're my assistant or something."

Noah smiled and Jonah laughed a little.

"I don't think I'm really cut out for the jungle life. Or the assistant life," Jonah said.

"Come on, little brother. It's not like you don't have some free time on your hands."

"That's subtle."

"I was just joking."

"I will miss you though, Noah."

"I figured you would."

One of the countless House of Rome waiters inquired about dessert and, once declined, exchanged a check for the empty dinner plates. Noah reached for the bill, and Jonah gladly let him. The two split a taxi as far as Jonah's apartment. Noah stayed in the car as the driver took him eight more blocks to his place. Although neither knew it at the time, the two brothers would see one another again before sunrise.

CHAPTER 10

ROM meal preparation to parental responsibilities, the people of Duba, as in all Amarakaeri villages, shared everything. They also shared their few material possessions, including canoes. The largest canoe of the village, a thirty-foot dugout, could support the weight of eleven grown men without allowing water to wash over the sides. A sixteen-horsepower Briggs and Stratton peke-peke motor was fixed in the back of the boat where Memphis and Artone planned to alternate driving shifts the following day.

Throughout their four years in the jungle, Memphis and Abigail had purposely managed to refrain from accumulating any more than they could personally carry on their backs – or heads, as was the custom among the Duba women. Underneath a blue plastic tarp lying in the large canoe, Memphis packed two adult-sized camping backpacks, a smaller carry-on backpack of Abigail's, a long hollow bamboo pole containing Memphis's hunting bow and arrows and two spears, and two baskets full of departing gifts ranging from oranges and feathered crowns to sugar cane and beaded necklaces.

While the rest of the village dried off from the group swim and prepared to go to sleep, Memphis rolled the sides of the tarp and tucked in the plastic to protect the baggage from potential rain. Standing on the makeshift dock where the canoe was securely tied, Memphis looked at the relatively small hump of things packed in the stern of the boat.

"I can't believe that everything we own fits under an old torn piece of plastic," he said aloud to himself.

"You're not talking to the fish again, are you?" Abigail asked.

Startled, Memphis turned to her.

"You could be a good hunter, sneaking up like that," Memphis said.

"I wasn't sneaking."

"No?"

"I was thinking."

"About what?"

"I was just thinking about the word 'downriver,'" Abigail said.

"What do you mean?"

"Well, ever since God called us to the jungle, we've been progressively moving upriver. The entire time it took us to discover the Amarakaeri and Duba, we traveled against the current. Now, after four years, we're one night away from going downriver."

"Downriver," Memphis repeated.

"Yes, downriver. I've got to say, I sure do like the sound of that. It's symbolic, don't you think?"

"Symbolic of what?" Memphis asked.

"Of home. Whenever I hear the phrase, downriver, I think of home."

Memphis wrapped his arm around Abigail who then tilted her head back, leaning it on Memphis's shoulder. Uncharacteristic for so early in the month, the moon cast enough light on the river that even the most amateur motorist could navigate a boat through the night. The luminous moonlight washed out the breathtaking spread of stars that typically filled the dark blanket of sky over what had served as the Jones's backyard for nearly half a decade.

"Just think of it, Memphis. We're going home tomorrow."

"Yes we are. Two weeks in Knoxville with my folks, and then Christmas with your family in Dallas."

"Even though I'm going to miss Duba, the church here, and especially Jenny and Art, I'm honestly looking forward to a month of vacation in the States. A month without bugs."

"Without heat," Memphis added.

"Without sleeping on the floor."

"Without having to build a fire every time you want to eat."

"Without having to trek down to the river every time you want to wash clothes."

"A month of cold soft drinks and fast food."

"McDonald's hamburgers."

"Pepperoni and sausage pizza from Pizza Hut; with extra cheese, of course."

"A hot bath."

"Worship in English."

"Movies."

"Hot chocolate by the fire."

"A Christmas with an actual Christmas tree."

"A Christmas with family."

"A Christmas at home."

"And it's all just a four-day trip away," Memphis said.

"A four-day journey downriver."

Memphis squeezed Abigail tighter as they watched the slow current roll by.

"Budteré!" Artone motioned from the top of the hill for the two to come to the community hut.

"I think the church wants to say good-bye," Abigail said.

The Joneses had lived in Duba for two and a half years before Memphis had learned enough of the native dialect to share the stories of the Bible with the village. Once able, Memphis taught about God's creation, provision, justice, mercy, forgiveness, grace, salvation, and love through stories such as Cain and Able, Noah and the ark, Abraham and Isaac, Daniel and the lions, and Jesus and His disciples. Since then, five of the fourteen Duba families had believed the message, been baptized in the river, and begun to follow Jesus Christ. This fellowship of Christians, which included Artone and Jehené, the first believers of Duba, made up the indigenous church.

Nearly every night found the faithful church gathering together in order to sing praises, retell the Biblical stories, exchange testimonies of the Lord's involvement in their lives, and to pray with and for one another. It was a sweet expression of the love of Jesus, one that Memphis and Abigail prayed would prove contagious throughout the Amazon jungle.

Memphis and Abigail walked into the community hut where the church had often gathered to worship whenever it didn't meet in one of the homes. All five families waited, scattered about the hut. Some reclined in the hammocks hanging between the posts on the sides of the hut, while the rest sat contentedly on the ground. Jehené held Petpet in her arms. Abigail was pleased to see the baby not crying.

Upon the missionaries' entrance, non-stop tears, mainly among the women, and outbursts of laughter, mainly among the men, immediately followed. Reminiscing the good times – past hunting and fishing escapades and sweet nights of worship with the church – and imagining scenarios of a future reunion, the nostalgic group ushered in midnight before the families said their final good-byes. Four years earlier, the entire community had cast their votes against Memphis and Abigail, sentencing them to death. Now they forsook all cultural norms by hugging the two foreign friends with a strong mixture of strength and sentiment.

Artone led the church in a prayer that seemed to bring the Body of Christ directly into the presence of God. After singing a song of praise in the Duba dialect, Harakmbut, and praying for the missionaries' upcoming journey, the group dispersed. Artone and Jehené stayed until the end.

As the final family faded into the darkness down the trail and Petpet could barely be seen riding in a blanket tied around his mother's shoulders and neck, Memphis and Abigail lingered in the community hut where they sat quietly in front of the dying fire. A few coals continued to burn. Memphis threw one more log onto the fire, blowing the coals in order to resurrect the waning flames. A lone tear streamed out of the corner of his eye.

"Is that tear for the church or from the smoke in your eyes?" Abigail asked. Sitting next to Memphis, she affectionately watched him through the faint light the fire shed on his face.

"I'm just going to miss it all so much," he said, barely able to form the words.

An hour later, Memphis and Abigail stood up from the fire and retired to their hut for the last time. Crawling into their mosquito net, which they habitually tucked under their sleeping mats once inside, the two cuddled in their giant sleeping bag and fell asleep within minutes.

CHAPTER 11

*I*N the jungle, signs in the sky rather than numbers on a clock measure the passing of time. When the sun rises, it's time to go to work. When the sun is directly above, it's time to go eat. When the sun causes the sky to change colors to a bright orange and light purple, evening is approaching and it's time to walk back to the village. Once the stars appear, everyone should go to sleep. No one in Duba ever used numbers to refer to the time. In fact, apart from Memphis and Abigail, most had no clue that such things as hours and minutes and seconds existed.

Therefore, when tragedy hit, Memphis could not even venture a guess as to what hour it had all occurred.

"Budteré! Budteré!" The endless, desperate shouts could be heard from the other side of the river. Artone frantically screamed for Memphis while crying aloud prayers in Harakmbut as he ran down the trail leading to Memphis and Abigail's hut.

"Budteré! Petpet huamatinoea'eri, dakhue', dakhue' ee'!"

Memphis! Petpet is sick, incredibly sick!

His prayer reached the sleeping ears of the missionaries and within seconds Memphis and Abigail had abandoned their mosquito nets, encountering a swarm of confusion as Artone reached their hut yelling faster than they had ever heard him speak before. Memphis grabbed Artone's shoulder and firmly asked him to speak slower. Artone stopped and repeated all he had said. This time, Memphis understood. Artone burst into tears, falling to his knees, his face touching the dirt of the ground.

"What's happening?" Abigail asked Memphis.

"Petpet is unconscious," he said.

Right then, Jehené emerged from the dark with her baby in her hands. Hopeless, Jehené fell into Abigail's arms, the seemingly lifeless baby squished between them. Abigail spoke gently to her friend, but Jehené was inconsolable. While Abigail held her, she felt Petpet's wrist and examined his pulse.

"He has a pulse," she said to Memphis.

Memphis stepped out of the hut with their backpacks. He compassionately lifted Artone from the ground.

"Kee' e'mepuk," he said. *It's going to be alright.*

Awakened by Artone's screams, most of the men and women of the village now stood outside, close enough to hear what was going on. Immersed in silent prayers, Memphis, Abigail, Artone, and Jehené hurried down to the river where they quickly boarded the boat. Within seconds, the rope was untied, the motor started, and the boat headed downriver. The rest of the village watched from above, uncertain of anything.

While Abigail monitored Petpet's vital signs and symptoms, Memphis determinedly navigated the dark river, depending on moonlight for sight. In order to maximize the speed of the boat, Memphis struggled to make the best reads of the changing current, charting his course down the middle of the river where the current was swiftest. Traveling only when the sun was up, the trip from Duba to Manu, the closest community with any sort of staffed medical care, required a full four days on the river. Memphis looked at Petpet lying motionlessly in his mother's arms, and feared that he would not survive the night.

As Memphis drove the boat and Abigail treated the baby, the distressed parents wept quietly. Artone sat across from Memphis at the back of the canoe. For the first six hours of the journey, Artone rarely moved as he sat hunched over, his eyes fixed on the boat floor. His wife, exhausted from crying, stared into the river, questioning the effectiveness of her prayers.

Around nine in the morning, Artone offered to drive for a while and Memphis took the opportunity to walk to the front of the boat for a closer look at the motionless patient. Abigail updated him on the baby's vitals. No change had taken place. Memphis checked Petpet all over, trying, as Abigail had repeatedly done, to drip water from his finger into the baby's mouth.

"He's definitely dehydrated by now," he whispered to Abigail. "He desperately needs an IV."

"How quickly do you think we can get to Manu?" Abigail asked.

"We're actually making good time, and the motor is running smoothly, so it's possible that we could get there in about forty more hours. That's if we don't stop at all tonight."

"We have to keep going, Memphis."

"I know. Art and I will alternate shifts of driving and sleeping, while you and Jenny take turns sleeping and watching over Petpet."

Noon came and went without even the thought of food, but by mid-afternoon, everyone was hungry. Jehené, having just woken from her nap, cut the peel off of four oranges. Abigail waited for Jehené to finish eating, and then she handed Petpet back to his mother, trading the baby for an orange. Memphis returned to the helm, eating as he drove. Artone had recovered from his initial shock, and, as he ate, he talked with Memphis about Petpet's illness, probable diagnosis, possible treatment, and God's ability to heal.

"Apag e'nokbahuad' Petpet," Memphis reassured. *God has all the power to heal Petpet.*

In the front of the boat, Abigail held Jehené's hands that cradled Petpet. In broken dialect, Abigail prayed aloud with Jehené, asking God to heal the unconscious baby. An hour later, Abigail took her turn at a nap.

As the sun tucked itself into the western horizon, setting colorfully behind the jungle forest and the giant kapok trees, a familiar sound, growing louder and louder, could be heard over the loud peke-peke motor. The sound was downriver but rapidly approaching. Memphis quickly switched with Artone who resumed driving.

With his pocketknife drawn, Memphis flipped the blade open and, balancing on the side of the boat, walked to the very tip where the blue plastic covered all the bags. Without hesitation, Memphis sliced the tarp down the middle and forcefully pulled one side up, releasing the entire piece of plastic.

"Use this to cover you two and Petpet," he said to Abigail who was now awake, aware of the approaching situation.

Abigail took the tarp and draped it securely over Jehené and Petpet. The three huddled tightly together beneath the plastic. Memphis stood in the tip of the canoe and looked ahead downriver. A white wall of rain, stretching from bank to bank, moved upriver toward the boat. The drops hitting the river created a rumbling noise that sounded more like thunder than rain.

"It'll be here soon," Memphis said. He began to walk on the edge of the boat again, returning to the back.

Moments later, the boat and everything in it was soaked. The heavy shower engulfed the traveling party as Artone navigated the canoe through the densest part of the rainstorm. Only those sitting under the tarp stayed dry, and soon, Memphis and Artone were shivering from the cold. Abigail foresaw the chill the mixture of the pelting drops and intense wind would bring, and, therefore, abandoned her protective plastic. Rummaging through the two camping backpacks, now, along with all the exposed bags, drenched with water, Abigail located two rain jackets. Memphis met Abigail in the middle of the boat.

"Give one to Art," she said, having to yell in order for him to hear her over the fierce, crashing rain.

"Thanks, Babe," Memphis said.

Abigail ducked back beneath the tarp. Memphis and Artone put on the warm rain jackets, zipping them up all the way, and for twelve hours, both the rain and the vital trip continued. Every three hours, the men would switch, allowing the driver to rest, though not sleep, as he was needed to scoop water out of the steadily filling boat. The women rested fitfully throughout the night, though Petpet's condition kept them both greatly preoccupied. At six the following morning, the rain finally stopped.

Leftover rain clouds in the overcast sky blocked the rising sun. Memphis and Artone knowingly looked at one another, both welcoming the clouds that would most likely ensure a cool morning on the tranquil river. More than twenty-four hours had passed since they fled Duba. The rainstorm had slowed their pace, but not significantly, and Memphis remained optimistic, predicting that they would dock in Manu by midnight. They would have to find and waken doctors and nurses, but Memphis knew he would do whatever it took to guarantee Petpet the best medical attention possible.

"Memphis! He's awake!" Abigail shouted.

Jehené was sleeping while Abigail held Petpet in her tired arms. Without even taking time to interpret to Artone what Abigail had said, Memphis sprinted to the front of the boat. Artone continued to drive.

"I was just holding him, trying to get some drops of water into his mouth, and all of the sudden, I looked down, and he was looking back at me," Abigail said.

Memphis examined the baby's eyes and vital signs.

"He still has some yellow in his eyes, but not as much as before," Memphis said.

Petpet began to cry, waking Jehené, and pleasantly surprising both parents. Artone, still driving, stood to see the baby. Jehené rubbed Petpet's face caringly, sharing his tears.

"Praise God," Abigail said.

"E'todihue' Apag," Memphis repeated in Harakmbut.

"E'todihue' Apag!" Artone shouted. "E'todihue' Apag!"

"E'todihue' Apag," Jehené whispered in between sniffs brought on by her joyful tears.

Cries of praise to their Lord and Healer fell off their lips like beautiful songs of grateful adoration.

"He still needs to get to the doctor as soon as possible," Memphis said. "He needs an IV and medication."

"How much longer?" Abigail asked.

"We may make it before midnight," Memphis said. Memphis kissed the baby on the forehead, smiled at Jehené, and started walking toward the back of the boat.

"Keep praying," Abigail said as Memphis sat down across from Artone.

"I will."

CHAPTER 12

*I*n less than an hour after returning to his apartment, Noah was asleep. Jonah, on the other hand, was still wide-awake at eleven that night. With four glasses of wine in his system, Jonah was beginning to forget his terribly upsetting day. Just to be certain a few memories didn't slip past the wine, Jonah settled into his recliner with a bottle of whiskey.

From Jonah's dead apartment, life could be heard in the street below. There was talking and laughing, foot-traffic and cars whipping by, and a dim mixture of music emanating from a variety of nightclubs. Lights shone through the windows of Jonah's apartment and he couldn't help but think about the host of parties that were surely taking place all over New York City. He imagined married couples dancing and college students drinking. He could picture pubs with live music and stadiums with live games. Jonah wondered if Autumn, the Starbucks barista, was out there somewhere, lost in the night, melting a million hearts with her engaging eyes and flirtatious personality.

Jonah even remembered Mitch, his gifted, annoying student, and speculated as to his Friday night whereabouts. Did he have a date? Was he dazzling audiences with some impromptu open reading at an obscure coffee shop? Was Mitch with Autumn tonight?

Suddenly, the numbing effects of the alcohol wore off, giving place to insecurity, depression, and loneliness. Jonah reached for his phone.

The line on the other end rang twelve times before someone answered. The voice sounded disturbed and drowsy. Jonah had plainly awakened her.

"Paige, I need to talk to someone," Jonah confessed.

"Jonah? Is that you again? Do you know what time it is?"

"Actually, I don't."

"It's after midnight."

"Were you sleeping?" he asked.

"Yes. Can we talk later?"

"I got fired today, Paige."

"Is that why you called me from your office this morning?"

"No, I got fired after I talked to you."

"Why did you get fired, Jonah?" Paige asked, sounding almost sincere.

"They fired me because I can't write anymore."

Paige discerned that Jonah was searching for reassurance and confidence. She meant to give him neither. She had tried without ceasing during their marriage and for years after their divorce.

"Jonah, you've been drinking – and I don't just mean today. You know that you still can write. I know that you can write. You just need some inspiration."

"Yes! Paige, you have spoken correctly. What I need is inspiration. I need to be stimulated with thought. Motivated with words. Awakened by language."

"You're going to be fine, Jonah. I will talk to you later."

Paige moved to hang-up the phone, but Jonah snuck in one last word that led to a few more.

"Paige, did you mean what you said today?"

"What did I say, Jonah?" Paige asked through a long yawn.

"You said I was a lonely drunk with incurable writer's block."

"Jonah, I was upset. I always get upset when you call me while you're drunk."

"So do you think that I'll write again?"

Honestly, Paige did not know what she believed. Was Jonah simply in a slump, or was he the epitomé of washed-up talent? The answer, of course, would not be found tonight. Paige's goal was to end the phone call so that she could go back to sleep.

"Of course you'll write again, Jonah," she said with little conviction.

"Don't patronize me, Paige. I hear nothing but doubt and

mockery in your voice. Doubt and mockery, Paige!"

"Well what would you have me say, Jonah? It's the middle of the night and you're drunk."

"I want you to tell me the truth."

"OK, fine. I have my doubts that you will ever publish your great novel. At one time you were very talented and motivated, but perhaps that time has passed. You must move on before you waste the next twenty years sitting in front of a blank computer screen."

"Forget you, Paige!" Jonah yelled into the mouthpiece. He pitched the cordless phone like a fastball across the room, where it hit the wall and shattered into pieces.

Paige closed her eyes, willing herself to take deep breaths, and was asleep again within minutes.

Just before one o'clock, Jonah opened his refrigerator door. The light from inside was the only light in the apartment. He selected two beers and went into his bedroom. Less than fifteen minutes later, Jonah had emptied both bottles. He stumbled to a small desk in the corner of his room, and pulled two albums from a deep drawer.

Jonah and Paige's wedding album was one of the few items Paige did not contest during the divorce. She was more than happy to rid herself of all proof that the two were ever united. Jonah cried as he slowly flipped through all 120 pages of photographs. He wept for his late parents and for the young, spirited writer standing at the altar. He wept for his lovely bride, and for the life that he had squandered. He blamed himself for driving Paige away. When he had thoroughly dwelled upon the final image, Jonah was emotionally drained.

He picked up the other album and walked into the kitchen.

With a beer in his hand, Jonah sat at the kitchen table. The other album was a collection of various writing clips Jonah's mother had cut out of publications to save. Every page was a memory of a season in Jonah's life when he was gifted, productive, respected, and fulfilled; a season when Jonah had the capability to craft his future into anything he dreamed. Having wept at the sight of the wedding photos, Jonah cursed the old stories that now mocked him.

Finishing his beer, Jonah was instantly inspired.

He opened his laptop computer, launched Microsoft Word, and began to type. His fingers had not moved so quickly and freely in years. Just as in years past, words flowed effortlessly from his mind to the screen, filling a page in less than ten minutes. Jonah saved the document.

Save as? The computer asked.

"Suicide Letter," Jonah typed.

Jonah staggered to the bathroom connected to his bedroom. Opening the medicine cabinet, he selected two prescription medicine bottles. Both were painkillers, and pain was exactly what Jonah was determined to kill.

He passed through the dark apartment, reread the letter he had just typed for Noah, and, grabbing a brand new bottle of whiskey, left his apartment. Around the corner were three garages, one of them his. Jonah had paid an extra $100 a month in order to have a fully enclosed garage, and he was about to get his money's worth.

After Jonah clicked a small black button attached to his keychain, the metal garage door opened. He unlocked the driver's door of his truck and slouched his body inside. Clicking the black button again, the garage door shut. As it did, Jonah started the engine. He inserted an old, mixed CD that he and Paige used to dance to. Then, he began to take the pills.

There were nine pills remaining in the first bottle, and he swallowed them all with shots of whiskey. The second bottle was full, but Jonah only took six, because he didn't like the taste of the pills when mixed with liquor. The fumes from the exhaust filled the cramped garage. Jonah, noticing his sudden trouble in breathing, lay down on the front seat, falling asleep to a familiar song.

Twenty minutes after passing out, Jonah woke up coughing and trembling. Filled with desperation, he pressed the little black button as he rolled out of the truck and onto the garage floor. Through terrible pain, he crawled to the garage opening, and, for a moment, he stood up. The moment the cold wind blew by, though, Jonah went into convulsions, and fell forward onto the pavement. The driver of a gray Suburban slammed on his brakes, coming to a stop only inches from Jonah's pale face.

The Suburban driver dialed 911 on his cell phone while his wife covered Jonah with a blanket from the backseat. Paramedics arrived promptly, lifted Jonah onto a rolling cot, loaded him into the ambulance and rushed him to the emergency room. Meanwhile, police searched the garage, the truck, and even Jonah's apartment. The letter to Noah was still open on the computer screen, and, after locating Jonah's cell phone on his nightstand in the bedroom, Officer Wilkins browsed Jonah's recent calls list and then phoned Noah.

At the hospital, an automatic door flew open and the paramedics wheeled Jonah into the emergency room. Dr. Lance Franklin immediately appeared, asking the paramedics a memorized list of questions.

"Was any drug paraphernalia found?" One of the paramedics handed Dr. Franklin the two painkiller bottles the police discovered inside the truck.

"Did he mix the drugs with alcohol?"

"Whiskey," a paramedic replied.

"What are his symptoms?"

"Coughing, convulsions, fever, pale face."

"Age?"

"According to his license, he's thirty, doctor."

"He needs a gastric lavage," Dr. Franklin said.

Nurses were hurrying around the room, gathering needles and tubes and medication while the doctor prepped the near-death patient. Dr. Franklin inserted a flexible tube up Jonah's nose, down his throat, and into his stomach. All contents of the stomach were then suctioned out through the tube. Next, in order to rinse out the stomach, Dr. Franklin injected a saline solution into the tube and then suctioned it back out.

An older nurse injected medication into Jonah's arm to stimulate urination and defecation, while another, younger nurse with a mole on her cheek, inserted an IV needle filled with dextrose into a vein on the back of Jonah's hand. Both treatments were meant to further flush out all drugs from his system, and re-establish a balance of fluids and minerals in Jonah's body.

No painkillers were administered and, for an hour, Jonah was in excruciating pain, enduring the greatest misery of his life. His stomach was pumped, his blood extracted for testing, and his body injected. In addition to the endless procedures, the effects of fifteen painkillers coupled with wine, beer, and whiskey, took time to subside. After the preliminary procedures were complete and it was certain that Jonah's life had been spared and that he was not going to die that night, the nurses wheeled Jonah to a private room where he was allowed to rest.

Although Noah had arrived at the hospital at three-thirty in the morning, receiving frequent updates from Dr. Franklin on Jonah's condition, it was several hours before the hospital staff allowed him to see Jonah.

"I think it would be alright for you to visit with your brother now, Mr. Frost," Dr. Franklin said.

Noah was sitting in the waiting room where he had slept the night before.

"Thank you, doctor," Noah said.

Noah walked down the hall to Jonah's room. Outside the closed door, Noah fought tears that came with the thought of the frailty of his little brother's life the night before. What was he thinking? Noah wondered. And what am I supposed to say to him? For the first time in years, Noah prayed for his brother.

CHAPTER 13

THE final six hours on the boat proved the most difficult, as the lingering clouds darkened the night sky. The bright moonlight of the previous evening seemed a distant memory. Memphis tried having Abigail sit on the prow for a while, shining two bright flashlights on the dark waters, but that only served to further hinder their line of sight.

With the flashlights turned off, Abigail continued to sit on the prow, squinting through the murky night in an effort to see any obstructions in the river. Thick logs, fallen trees, hidden limbs, and shallow waters that could easily land the boat on a bed of rocks or sandy beach, all waited quietly and invisibly around each bend, threatening to flip the fragile canoe. Fortunately, no such accident took place and, at a quarter past midnight, the exhausted crew docked in Manu.

The community of Manu, located on the Madre de Dios River, is primarily a tourist town. Twelve months a year, tour groups from around the world traveled to Manu to pay thousands of dollars for a four-day voyage into the native jungle in hopes of spotting parrots and jaguars and, perhaps, meeting a real-life tribal people group. Along with the posh tourist lodges and American-style shops, which sell Snickers, Doritos and Coke, Manu also houses a dozen Peruvian families, a small school, and one medical center.

Memphis tied the boat to a heavy log lying on a hill of sandbags while Artone and Jehené rushed up a dozen concrete stairs with the crying baby wrapped tightly in a blanket. Abigail patiently waited at the dock while Memphis secured the canoe. A firm knot later, Memphis took Abigail's hand and they walked quickly to catch up with their friends.

Except for a table full of drunks laughing loudly in the doorway of the only open bar, the community looked like a ghost town. Artone was knocking on the locked door of the Centro de Salud when Memphis and Abigail caught up. Abigail joined Jehené on a bench outside the center.

"E'huapok e'kubere," Memphis said to Artone. *I'm going to go get help.*

Artone conceded and quit his hopeless knocking. He sat down on the other side of Jehené. After inconveniencing three obviously bothered men, Memphis learned the name and address of the practicing doctor: Dr. Esteban Roberts. To find him, go past the cows grazing behind the school, walk the trail through the field of banana trees, and then veer off the trail and head to the third hut on the left. Following these directions, Memphis ran to the hut.

Finding no door, Memphis simply knocked on the widest wooden post he could find. Impatiently, he knocked three times, and then began to holler.

"Señor Roberts," he called. "Señor Roberts. Tenemos una emergencia! We have an emergency!" Memphis alternated between Spanish and English.

"Necesitamos tu ayuda! We need your help! Please hurry! De prisa, por favor!"

A flashlight clicked on inside the hut. Wearing a pair of black mesh shorts, a man in his forties stepped into the doorway. He had short black hair with a fair share of gray mixed in. Flustered and confused, he put on his glasses and inspected his intruder. Any stranger who showed up unannounced at your house in the middle of the night, screaming, was an intruder, according to Dr. Roberts.

"¿Qué pasa?" He demanded brusquely. *What's happening?*

"Señor Roberts, soy Memphis Jones, hay un bebé enfermo que necesita ayuda," Memphis said. *There is a sick baby that needs help.*

"Are you an American, Memphis?" Dr. Roberts asked.
"Yes."
"Me too. Steven Roberts. We can speak English."
Dr. Roberts grabbed a T-shirt and a key.
"Lead the way," he said. "We'll talk as we walk."
Memphis and Dr. Roberts walked single file down the trail,

past the cows, around the school, and back to the Centro de Salud.

"What's wrong with your baby?" Dr. Roberts asked.

"He's not my baby. My wife and I are missionaries, and we've been living in a small village further up Manu River."

"Memphis. The baby?"

"Sorry. The baby, Petpet is his name, has been sick nearly his entire life. Recently, his symptoms have been a high fever, itching, yellow eyes, vomiting, and dark-red urine. I gave him medicine to stop the vomiting and treat malaria, but two nights ago, he fell unconscious. We left immediately and traveled more than forty hours non-stop to get here tonight. Earlier this morning, Petpet woke up, and has been crying ever since. He's most likely dehydrated."

"Well, we'll have a look at him. Are his parents here?"

"Yes, Artone and Jehené."

"Do they speak Spanish?"

"No, just their native dialect. But I can translate."

"Good. That's pretty lucky that the baby woke up."

"Not lucky, Doctor; a miracle."

The doctor cynically looked at Memphis as they rounded a corner to the Centro de Salud. Jehené immediately stood and tried to hand the baby to Dr. Roberts. He handed Petpet back to Jehené, and motioned for her to wait. Walking up the steps to the door, Dr. Roberts unlocked the building, entered, and flipped on a light switch. The light revealed a simple office and three small patient rooms, divided by sliding curtains, each complete with a bed and various medical supplies.

Artone and Jehené had never seen a doctor's office and did not know what to do. They stood in the doorway as Dr. Roberts opened one of the curtains and began making preparations in the room. Abigail took the baby from Jehené and gestured for the puzzled parents to follow. Abigail laid Petpet on the table, gently holding him in place. The baby continued to cry as he had since first waking. As the others prayed and watched, Dr. Roberts examined the baby, asking questions from time to time. Memphis answered when he knew, and translated both question and response when he did not.

"Well, the yellow in the white of his eyes and the itching, seem to point toward jaundice," Dr. Roberts said as he took the baby's temperature. "Often, jaundice is a symptom of malaria, and when accompanied by the high fever, vomiting, and dark-red urine, malaria does, indeed, seem likely."

"And the unconsciousness?" Abigail asked.

"There are a few cases of Falciparum Malaria in which unconsciousness occurs," Dr. Roberts explained.

"Falciparum?" Abigail asked.

"It's a more serious case of malaria," Dr. Roberts responded. "It is often fatal."

Memphis and Abigail looked at one another. No one translated for Artone and Jehené.

"I'm going to need a urine sample and a blood smear," Dr. Roberts said. "Perhaps you could wait with the parents outside," he suggested to Abigail. "Memphis, I could use your assistance."

Abigail complied, leading Artone and Jehené into another room. Sitting together, the three held hands, and took turns praying for the health and recovery of Petpet throughout the remainder of the night. At five in the morning, Memphis opened the curtain to the room where Abigail, Artone, and Jehené sat waiting. Abigail looked up at Memphis.

"The urinalysis showed positive blood and protein," he said.

"The first blood smear came back negative, but Dr. Roberts said that's because the malaria parasites often get stuck in the tiny blood vessels. Apparently, it's common for the blood examined to appear free of malaria though it is not."

"So it is malaria," Abigail said.

"The second blood smear returned positive," Memphis said.

Dr. Roberts entered the room, holding Petpet in his arms. He gave the baby to Jehené.

"Petpet has a form of malignant malaria," he said. "It's a severe case that usually leads to death; especially when the patient has been unconscious."

Memphis slowly translated the diagnosis to Artone and Jehené who required much more explanation, as the medical terms were completely lost in the translation. Once they understood, Memphis nodded at Dr. Roberts and he continued.

"I have treated Petpet with Quinine to combat the malaria. He's going to need to stay in bed for a few days. We will monitor his vital signs every two hours. Also, I'm going to hook him up to an IV to hydrate him."

"Thank you so much, Doctor," Abigail said.

"Yes, thank you," Memphis repeated.

Memphis told Artone and Jehené that they would need to stay in Manu for a few days with Petpet. He also said that he and Abigail would wait with them. This pleased Artone, who was uncomfortable staying in a community where he could not communicate with anyone. Dr. Roberts lay Petpet on the bed, started his IV, and routinely recorded the baby's vitals. Following the previous two sleepless nights, Memphis and Artone began to feel extremely fatigued. Since the Center only had two other beds, Artone and Jehené slept near their child, while Memphis and Abigail found a room at a lodge not thirty yards away.

By eight thirty, two nurses had taken over the care of the patient, and Dr. Roberts had retired to his hut to catch up on lost sleep. Before allowing him to leave though, Artone and Jehené had bombarded him with hugs. Jehené kissed both of his hands repeatedly.

Following several hours of much-needed sleep, Memphis, Abigail, Artone, and Jehené found a small restaurant where they each devoured a bowl of hot soup and a plate of fried catfish and rice. Full and rested, the four relaxed at the table for a couple of hours after cleaning their plates. They reviewed the worries and dangers of the past three days as well as the answered prayers.

By the next morning, the nurses pronounced Petpet completely healed, and, by that afternoon, Dr. Roberts released the patient. He gave a bag of medicine to Artone who received second-hand instructions from Memphis on how to administer the treatment. While Artone and Jehené wrapped Petpet in blankets, Memphis and Abigail walked outside the Centro de Salud.

"Are they going to start upriver today?" Abigail asked.

"Yeah, I think Art wants to get back home as soon as possible."

"Speaking of home, I guess we'll be leaving soon, too."

"Sooner than you think."

"What do you mean?"

"There's a plane bringing in a group of tourists tonight. It will land at eight o'clock at the Manu airport on the other side of the river. An hour later, you and I will board a flight to Lima. We'll be in Tennessee late tomorrow."

"Tomorrow?" Abigail threw herself into Memphis's arms.

"Do we have a boat to take us across the river?" Abigail asked.

"The tour agent that's going to pick up his tour group from the airport will give us a ride. We'll leave as soon as Art and Jenny do. Then, we'll enjoy four wonderful weeks of vacation in the States before we begin our new mission."

"When do we come back?"

"We'll fly back into Peru the day after Christmas. I hope we make as good friends in the next village as we did in Duba."

"Oh, no," Abigail said.

"What, Babe?"

"It just hit me. We're going to have to say goodbye to Jenny and Art."

Artone and Jehené walked out of the Centro de Salud with Petpet. They all began talking at once as they slowly walked to the docks. Artone and Memphis laughed as they relived a past hunting trip when the entire hunting party, about twelve men, had trapped several wild pigs. In silence, they had waited. Just before they made their move, the herd was startled by a loud outburst of laughter from behind a large cedar tree. Every single pig had escaped and the entire community had held Memphis and Artone responsible. Even then, with the entire hunting party angry, Memphis and Artone had been unable to stop laughing. They had laughed all the way back to the village. Years later, the story made them laugh all over again.

Abigail and Jehené talked about the miraculous healing of Petpet and how, one day, they hoped that Memphis and Abigail could come back to Duba to visit. They all smiled at the thought of Petpet and Memphis Jr. climbing trees together.

Faster than they wanted to, the two families arrived at

the Manu docks. Memphis kissed Jehené's cheek and Artone kissed Abigail's. Abigail and Jehené hugged one another and prayed together, prolonging their goodbye for another half hour. Neither wanted to let go.

Jehené was the first Amarakaeri woman to give her life to Jesus and the first Amarakaeri woman to give her friendship to Abigail. The Lord had knit their hearts together, blessing the two women with a bond stronger than even the closest of sisters. Abigail couldn't stop shaking as her Jenny prayed. It didn't seem too long ago that Jehené said her first prayer, and yet, the act of praying together was as familiar as the trail from Abigail's hut to Jenny's.

Memphis and Artone quietly stood next to each other, watching the boats on the river. Finally, the two men said their goodbyes without saying a word. Each placed his right palm over his heart and then touched the heart of the other. Fighting tears, the men embraced.

CHAPTER 14

QUIETLY, Noah opened the door. Jonah lay in a hospital bed connected to tubes, IVs, and machines. His face was swollen and bruised from his fall on the street. Dried blood painted a considerable part of his face due to a nosebleed caused by the tubing. Stretches of purple on his arms and hands revealed the places where nurses had injected medicine and extracted blood.

A bucket of ice chips sat on a tray an arm's length from

the bed. After having his stomach pumped and five sessions of induced vomiting, Jonah's throat hurt worse than any of the other injuries. Although the ice chips were meant to comfort his soreness, they did not.

Following a hellish night of pain, Jonah was sleeping.

Noah tried to compose himself as he digested the horrific scene. He had never seen his brother so beat up, so hurt, so low. Noah, wearing his emotions on his sleeve, began to pace the cold room.

To occupy his mind, Noah briefly read Jonah's chart, which was hanging on a clipboard magnetically attached to the footboard of the bed. Unable to understand the chicken-scratch handwriting and the medical gibberish, Noah returned the chart and continued to pace.

"What time is it?" Jonah painfully asked in a hoarse, strained voice. He had awakened and his voice sounded as though he had just drunk a bottle of hard liquor for the first time; or, perhaps, as if he had recently had a tube stuck down his throat in order to suck an overdose of drugs out of his stomach.

"It's a little before seven," Noah said. "Don't talk right now, though, Jonah. You need to rest your voice; allow it to heal."

Jonah nodded, rubbing his eyes as they adjusted to the morning sunlight entering through the window. He attempted to sit up.

"Relax, Jonah. You need your rest."

Noah sat in a green, cushioned chair facing the bed, staring at his brother with compassion, anger, pity, and confusion.

"When did you get here?" Jonah asked in a barely audible whisper.

"About three hours ago," Noah replied. "The police found

my number on your cell phone."

"Oh."

"They found my name first, though, on your computer screen."

"Oh."

Jonah shut his eyes with regret and rolled onto his side, his back toward Noah.

"Did you read the letter?" Jonah hesitantly asked.

"No, Jonah. I came straight here. Your computer is still in your apartment."

"Good."

"So I'm guessing you don't want me to read it now."

"No."

"Does that mean that you've changed your mind about whatever it was that you wrote and attempted last night?"

"Noah, I just wanted the pain to go away."

An overflow of tears swelled in the corners of Noah's eyes and began streaming down his face.

"Jonah, you know that suicide will never make anything better. No pain can be healed by more pain."

"I don't even know that I was really trying to kill myself, Noah." Jonah rolled to his other side so that he could face Noah. Upon seeing his brother's tears, Jonah, too, began to cry.

"Jonah, you overdosed on drugs that you took with whiskey. Then, you locked yourself in your garage and started your truck. What did you think was going to happen?"

"I don't remember what I was thinking. I don't remember much of anything from last night."

"Did you call Paige?"

"I think so."

Noah took his brother's bruised, cold hands and placed them in his own.

"I know what it's like to go through a divorce, Jonah. And I know that sometimes it seems like everything in the whole world is geared toward making every aspect of your life absolutely miserable. It feels like unseen forces are fighting against you."

"Yes, Noah, it does."

"But you have to fight back. You can't give up."

"I'm too tired to fight, and I don't think I know how to anymore, Noah. I haven't the slightest idea what I should do next."

"There's a multitude of things you should do, Jonah. You need to sober up, you need closure to your relationship with Paige, you need to escape the pressures of publishing for a while, and...you need to...live." Saying the last word, Noah burst into another set of tears. Jonah followed suit.

While the two brothers sat crying, a nurse walked into the room. Respectfully ignoring the emotion of the moment, she politely placed two small cups of medicine on the tray next to the ice chips, and switched IV's. Noah and Jonah watched in silence. After making a few marks on Jonah's chart, the nurse gave Jonah a sympathetic smile, and Noah a friendly one, and then left the room.

"So, big brother, how do you suppose I go about getting all those things you said that I need?" Jonah sincerely asked. "Do you think that I should join one of those Alcoholics Anonymous groups or something?"

"Maybe. I don't think it would hurt. You desperately need to quit drinking."

"This counselor came in here earlier with all of these pamphlets and brochures for a variety of groups. Did you know there are self-help groups for alcoholics as well as unemployed, depressed, suicidal, and divorced men? She had them all. I never knew I had so many problems until last night."

"Well, that's because you sort of hit bottom last night. Eight hours ago, you, Jonah Frost, reached the lowest point of your life."

"I know you haven't had much practice, but I've got to say, Noah, the counselor was much better at this than you, much more encouraging."

"Jonah, sometimes, to be at the bottom, the lowest of your days, can be very encouraging indeed."

"I'm not following your logic here."

"From this hospital bed, Jonah, you have nowhere to go but up; up to a better, healthier, more enjoyable, and worthwhile life."

"Life," Jonah laughed. "Look around Noah. My *life* has been shattered into a pile of meaningless pieces. There's just not that much to live for these days."

"Then let's discover some meaning. Let's find a life worth living. Let's find it together."

"What are you talking about, Noah? I'm the one who's all doped up, but you're not making any sense."

Noah stood. With the counselor's pamphlets in his hands, he walked across the room, thinking about the host of support groups. What was the best thing for Jonah? What was his role in helping his brother?

"Jonah, if you stay here, in the city, and continue to spend day after day sitting in front of your computer screen, torturing yourself, then you're right, there's not much to live for. However, if you forget all of it, the school, Paige, the novel, and go out there and live, experience an adventure, then maybe you'll discover a new and fulfilling life."

"And this adventure is going to solve my writer's block?"

"Your writer's block? I'm talking about your *life*. Forget the book. You almost died last night. Don't you get it? You need to make some significant changes. You have issues that aren't going to magically go away once you have a book sitting on a shelf at Barnes & Noble. Your greatest needs right now are not to write and publish, but to survive and live. And aside from all of that, I seriously do think that your current situation and the urgency for change that it demands, is intimately related to your writing, or lack thereof."

Noah's voice had abandoned compassion and embraced honesty. His voice was firm, his words piercing. It was the first time Noah had diminished the importance of Jonah's first book, while depreciating his ability to write it.

"How in the world do you think that by forsaking my novel and turning my life upside down, I will somehow overcome writer's block and once again write?" Jonah asked. "I can't even begin to see how the two are related."

"Jonah, ever since your divorce you have voluntarily secluded yourself to your apartment in utter isolation, forbidding yourself to experience life until you publish. It is an invented detachment that you foolishly view as discipline. I mean, did you ever think that, perhaps, the reason you are unable to write is because you have nothing to write about? No offense, Jonah, but no one wants to read a book about a drunk, isolated in his apartment, staring at a blinking cursor hour after hour.

"You are great with words, brother. I know you love to write. It's your passion and, therefore, without it, it's as if you've lost your very soul. But the words alone can't satisfy you.

They won't fulfill you. Though you may have the words, what you desperately need to take hold of is life itself – adventure, danger, and love. And in finding a life worth living, you might also uncover a story worth writing, a story worth reading, a story worth publishing."

Jonah leaned his head back and closed his eyes as he gradually became convinced of the validity of Noah's observation. As always, the truth was accompanied by fear and pain. Jonah looked into his brother's unwavering eyes.

"Where am I to find such a life, Noah? You think those support groups will give me adventure and danger and love?"

"You're going to come with me, Jonah. You're going to come with me to the Amazon jungle."

"You can't be serious."

"It's the perfect escape from alcohol, Paige, writing, and unemployment. You can spend the next two weeks meeting with some of these support groups, and then, the day after Christmas, we'll leave it all behind and start over."

"I appreciate the invitation, Noah, but...."

"It's not an invitation, Jonah. It's an intervention. You will come with me."

Jonah nodded in uncertain approval.

PART TWO

The
Isconahua

CHAPTER 15

STRETCHING his legs and using his hands to support his aching lower back as he stepped out of the taxi, Dr. Basil Cosgrove breathed deeply, taking in a refreshing breath of a familiar atmosphere. While it was Dr. Cosgrove's first time this far down the Madre de Dios River, he was by no means a rookie to the South American jungles. For the past nineteen years, the now aging anthropologist had journeyed outside of his homeland to the hidden villages of more than two dozen tucked-away native tribes.

He loved his job. He was good at his job. Well known and well respected in several areas of expertise, Dr. Basil Cosgrove was a visionary anthropologist with one assignment left in him. He had vowed to make it his most successful mission yet.

The taxi driver unloaded Basil's backpack from the trunk and gratefully received his payment with tip. Dust flew in the air, settling in Basil's white beard as the taxi sped away. Basil looked out over the river and the jungle traffic, observing all the business taking place two days after Christmas.

Bread vendors beckoned arriving and departing locals to buy their cheap, stale loaves. In front of the gold exchange, shirtless men with large bellies waited in line with tiny nuggets representing a month of hard labor. A group of eight sweaty men hauled heavy boards from their boat to the back of a large truck parked on the riverbank, while dozens of kids shed their clothes as they ran excitedly to play in the river. Gold-mining machines were roaring, roosters were crowing, and bananas were for sale at every store and restaurant. Dr. Basil Cosgrove was home.

Just before his enjoyment of his surroundings could reach its full potential of rich satisfaction, Basil's eyes landed on a young married couple talking to a Peruvian boat motorist near the river. Basil threw his backpack off his shoulders and onto the ground where he kicked it over a few times.

"Out of all the people in the world to be here today, these two had to show up," Basil said.

Noah and Jonah spent their Christmas vacation balancing preparations for their Peruvian jungle adventure with Jonah's numerous support groups. With a great deal of exhortation from Noah, Jonah managed to abstain from drinking any form of alcohol. Even the depression of a lonely Christmas day proved weaker than Jonah's resolve.

The day after Christmas, the Frost brothers flew to Lima, Peru. Early the next morning, the two men boarded a small plane to the jungle community of Puerto Maldonado, Peru. An hour before Dr. Cosgrove's taxi pulled into the river port located on the outskirts of Maldonado, Noah and Jonah's cab dropped them off by the same riverbank.

If their white skin and green eyes were not enough to single the Frost brothers out in the middle of a small Peruvian town, Noah and Jonah sported brand new camping clothes that drew attention and exposed them as outsiders and jungle first-timers. More than that, it led all who saw them to conclude that they were a couple of tourists.

They wore matching khaki pants with zippers on the knees

that gave them the option of turning their pants into shorts. Their long-sleeve, button-down camping shirts were equipped with mesh vents on the back and under the armpits, while their hiking boots shined like the gold being sold next door to the humble restaurant where they ate. Their passports hung around their necks, their hats betrayed their amateur jungle status, and Jonah unknowingly boasted two store tags on his shirt.

"They're not very strict about time around here are they?" Jonah observed.

Noah was finishing his breakfast, ripping with his teeth a last bite of the tough mystery meat on his plate. Jonah had previously given up on his meal without regret as it cost him only the equivalent of seventy-five cents.

"Yeah, I guess not," Noah agreed.

"That boat driver said he'd be ready to leave an hour ago." Jonah said. "Can you see him? What's he doing?"

"It looks like he's talking to a couple of Americans."

"You think he's going to take them with us?"

"I suppose it's a possibility," Noah said. "It would probably drop the price of renting the boat if a few more passengers came along."

Memphis was an expert bargainer. He had long forsaken the American concept of paying the asking price and learned to negotiate with any and all salesmen. If a Coke cost two dollars, he'd pay one. A new, five-dollar T-shirt was a buck fifty, and he'd get gas for ten percent off. Memphis refused to settle for the starting price of anything in Peru.

"I've already lowered my fee twenty percent for you," the Peruvian boat motorist objected.

Speaking Spanish like a true Peruvian, Memphis was fully engaged in the bargaining process as Abigail tried not to look embarrassed.

"There's no way I'm paying you one hundred dollars a day just to take us up river," Memphis fired back. "The only reason you're jacking up your price is because we're Americans. We're going to pay what any normal Peruvian would pay, Alejo."

Nearly a foot taller than Alejo, Memphis was quite intimidating. And he was not backing down. He took a step closer.

"I'll pay you fifty dollars a day," he said. "And that's just because the gas prices are up a bit right now."

"No one ever travels up river, Angosto," Alejo retorted. "You won't find anyone else to take you. I'm the only motorist willing to travel within one hundred kilometers of the Isconahua. Everybody else is scared of them."

"Why is it, Alejo, that you are not afraid?" Memphis asked.

"Oh, I am afraid," Alejo replied. "It's just that I need the money. Plus, I figure, you're white; if they decide to kill us, they'll kill you first. Maybe I'll have time to get away."

Memphis smiled. "You're very brave, Alejo."

"So it'll be seventy dollars a day for my bravery."

"If you don't take sixty a day, I'll leave now and look for someone else."

Alejo hesitated. Memphis glanced at another motorist and Alejo promptly extended his greasy hand. Memphis suspiciously shook it. He had learned not to be too quick to trust a Peruvian motorist.

There are three types of people when it comes to interest in foreign lands: There are those who long to travel the world and know other cultures. There are those who prefer to remain at home, but wish to look at pictures of far-off lands so they may feel they are cultured. And there are those who do not care about the person living next door, much less about someone on the other side of the world.

Grace Cervantes, a freelance photographer from Madrid, Spain, was the first type with hopes to fulfill the longings of the second type. Named after the famous actress, Grace Kelly, who lived and died just eleven hours from Madrid, Grace unknowingly inherited the elegance of her namesake as well as the adventurous spirit of her late father.

For Christmas this year, the best gift Grace received was the phone call from the most prominent travel magazine in Spain. The editor, familiar with some of her previously published work, offered to pay her expenses plus a respectable stipend if she would go to the Peruvian jungles for three months and photograph a newly located native tribe. Grace had screamed "Yes!" into the phone and was on a plane the next day. Now all she had to do was find someone to take her up the Piedras and Angosto Rivers.

Grace's Spanish was flawless and enabled her to search with ease up and down the river port for a ride. After more than twenty rejections from motorists who refused to enter the Isconahua territory, Grace noticed an American couple loading their backpacks into a fifteen-foot long, roofed boat. Expecting another rejection, she, with her backpack bouncing, hurriedly made her way to the docks.

CHAPTER 16

"*I* ASSUME that your presence here means that you have decided to terminate your mission to destroy the lives of the Duba savages," Dr. Cosgrove said without a hint of jesting.

Memphis spun around.

"Basil Cosgrove," he said. "I can't believe it."

"You can't believe it? You have no idea how my stomach turned the second I saw you today."

Basil crowded Memphis as a schoolyard bully would challenge his next victim. Memphis took a step forward placing his nose inches from Basil's red face.

"What are you doing here, Memphis?" Basil asked. "You're not planning on ruining any more savage cultures, are you?"

Memphis's anger stirred within his chest that was now unconsciously taking in deep breaths. Memphis thought about Artone and Jehené and Petpet.

"It's a funny thing, Basil," he began. "We never actually saw any savages. Just a tribe of friends."

"Friends? Well, how nice for you. You and your little wife made a few wild jungle friends at the mere cost of an entire way of life that is now polluted by your Christian beliefs."

Hearing his wife brought into the exchange, Memphis slightly pushed Basil in the chest with both hands, knocking him back a step.

"Is that the Christian love you preach?" Basil mocked.

Abigail moved into the space between her husband and Basil. She sternly looked Memphis in the eyes with a firm, yet compassionate stare of understanding.

"Which tribe are you hoping to turn into caged zoo animals this time?" Memphis asked as calmly as the situation permitted. "Whom do you want to study now?"

"I'm here to observe the Isconahua," Basil answered as he dusted Memphis's palm prints off his shirt.

"Well, that's where we're headed, but I don't think there are any more motorists that will take you up there."

Basil looked past Memphis and Abigail. Alejo was covering the Jones's and Jonah and Noah's backpacks with a blue plastic tarp.

"I'll pay you one hundred dollars a day to take me along with these Christians to see the Isconahua," Basil called out in Spanish to Alejo.

Memphis, knowing that no Peruvian motorist would turn down such an offer, dropped his head in defeated disapproval. Alejo ran up and shook Basil's hand and then grabbed the backpack and threw it into the boat. Dr. Cosgrove gave Memphis a sneering smile and then took his place in the last chair in the boat.

As Memphis squeezed Abigail's hand and prayed silently for patience and self-control, a young lady with a camera around her neck approached them.

"Excuse me," Grace began. She was as well-spoken in English as she was in Spanish. "My name is Grace Cervantes."

"Abigail Jones. This is my husband, Memphis."

The three new acquaintances shook hands.

"I'm a photographer with the *Mensajero* magazine in Madrid, Spain," Grace said. "I've been sent to take pictures of an indigenous people group only recently located on the Angosto River, the Isconahua. Are you familiar with this tribe or the river?"

Abigail smiled. Grace obviously had repeated this speech numerous times throughout the morning.

"Yes," Abigail said. "In fact, we're leaving today to contact the Isconahua in hopes of living with them."

"Are you anthropologists?"

"No, we're missionaries," Memphis said.

"Is there anyone here that could possibly take me to the Isconahua?" Grace asked.

Memphis stared into Grace's eyes. He prided himself on his discernment of a person's character. He had been right when he first met Dr. Basil Cosgrove, and he believed he was right about Grace Cervantes.

"I'll talk to Alejo, our motorist, and see if he will take you along with us," he said.

"That would be great," Grace said. "Thank you so much."

Memphis excused himself from the conversation and began to negotiate all over again with Alejo. Meanwhile, Abigail and Grace exchanged life stories within minutes, as women are known to do.

While Noah was reviewing their trip checklist, Jonah spotted the two ladies talking and stopped walking, frozen by the sight of Grace Cervantes.

She had on short, khaki shorts that revealed long, tan legs, and a forest-green tank top that showed just enough of her shoulders to make Jonah want to see more. Her hazel hair was put up in a ponytail, for the jungle was too hot to let it rest across her tower-like neck. With honey brown eyes and a captivating smile, Grace, with just one look, ruined Jonah's heart for anyone else. She was indisputably the most beautiful woman ever to invade his life.

"Jonah, seriously, she sees you staring," Noah said.

Jonah snapped out of his trance and looked up at his older brother, a moment too late to avoid detection. Grace was curiously staring back at Jonah. Noah led the embarrassed tourist over to the two pretty women.

"I apologize for my brother," Noah said as he approached Abigail and Grace. "It's his first time to the jungle."

"I can see that," Grace said, pulling a forgotten price tag off Jonah's brand new camping shirt. Everyone but Jonah laughed.

"Noah Frost," Noah said, extending his hand to the girls.

"Abigail Jones."

"Grace Cervantes."

"I'm Jonah," Jonah finally blurted out. "Jonah Frost. His brother. I'm sorry about earlier."

"Don't apologize," Grace said. "You'll ruin the flattering moment."

Jonah returned Grace's smile and, for the first time in nearly a decade, felt as though he could, between that second and the next, die satisfied for having lived a worthy life.

"Where are you two headed?" Abigail asked. "Are you on one of the jungle tours?"

"I suppose we do look a bit like tourists," Noah conceded.

"Just a bit," Abigail joked.

"Actually, though, I'm a linguist. Our institute discovered new information last month about a native tribe in this region that has yet to be contacted. I'm here to engage in preliminary language studies of their indigenous dialect."

"Interesting," Grace said, wondering if Noah's tribe might be the same one she had come to photograph. "And are you a linguist too?" she asked Jonah. "Is that why you are here?"

Jonah struggled for words and came up empty. What should he say? He hadn't thought about having to reveal his travel motives to complete strangers. Especially beautiful, sexy, foreign strangers. Should he just come right out and say, "Yeah, I sort of cracked up after my wife left, and my career hit rock bottom, then I got fired, and a few weeks ago, I got drunk and tried to kill myself, so my brother decided I needed an adventurous escape if I was to have a chance of surviving"?

Jonah looked at his brother and then at Grace and then Abigail and then Grace again, allowing himself to get lost in her eyes once more.

"I just thought I'd tag along with Noah," he lied. "I had some vacation time and I've always wanted to see the Amazon jungle, so I figured I'd make the trip and keep my big brother company."

Neither Abigail nor Grace believed a word of it.

"So I assume the indigenous tribe that you aim to study is the Isconahua," Abigail said to Noah.

"That's right," he said. "How did you know?"

"Well, apparently they are very popular all of a sudden," Abigail said.

"Linguist?" Noah asked looking at Grace.

"Photographer," she said, receiving a new look of interest from Jonah.

"Missionaries," Abigail said.

"Plural?"

"I'm here with my husband, Memphis," Abigail said, pointing toward Memphis who was wrapping up negotiations with Alejo.

"What about the old man in the boat?" Jonah asked.

"He's the thorn in my side," Memphis said as he joined the

group. He firmly shook Noah's hand and then Jonah's as only a self-confident man can do.

"Or, perhaps more appropriately put," Memphis continued, "he's an anthropologist that seems to be following us around."

Noah glanced at Basil and then refocused on Memphis. "So, why do they call you Memphis?" he asked.

"Because that's my name," Memphis answered.

"Right. I mean, were you born in Memphis, Tennessee?"

"Close. Knoxville. The name comes from my grandfather. He was an all-star pitcher for the Memphis Chicks back in the twenties."

"Who are the Memphis Chicks?" Jonah asked.

"That used to be the name of the city's minor league baseball team. My dad grew up hearing all of these stories about the Chicks, their one hundred wins in the 1921 season, and how my grandfather once pitched an entire game left-handed just to win a bet he had made with the catcher. My dad sort of fell in love with the stories and the team he never saw play. So when I was born, he was determined to keep the story going. I'm just glad he didn't name me Chicks."

Jonah and Noah laughed, welcoming Memphis's sense of humor, believing it would add to their trip. They shook Memphis's hand again, assuring him that it was their pleasure, and then made their way to Alejo's boat.

Memphis looked back over his shoulder as the Frost brothers walked away. Again, his eyes fell on Basil who was settled into his seat and was proceeding to review a file of research.

It would be a long trip indeed.

CHAPTER 17

RIPPLED by the motor's prop, the trailing water formed a V behind the boat, stretching out toward the parallel banks. Like a mirrored reflection, a flock of green, yellow and blue parrots flew in the same V-shape above the rocking wake. The two designs reflected one another until the birds broke off over the tree line.

Noah was quickly learning the basics of river navigation as Alejo taught him how to read the river and slightly steer the boat around each bend. Basil was settled into his chair, examining a file containing what little information had been gathered on the Angosto River and the allusive Isconahua. As if they were sisters, Abigail and Grace chatted away on the front bench near the bow of the boat.

Separated from the group by purpose, skill, and interest, Jonah sat on the left side of the middle seat with nothing to offer. He wasn't learning how to drive, he wasn't preparing for a job or mission with the Isconahua, and suddenly he was very uncomfortable with the ever-apparent truth that he had no reason whatsoever to be there. Water splashed into the boat, further annoying him. He wiped his wet hand on his pant leg and surveyed his surroundings.

Where in the world am I? He asked himself. I should be in New York drinking coffee and writing. Who am I kidding? I'd be drinking liquor and picking fights with Paige over the phone. I still don't see how this is going to do me any good – a couple of useless months in the jungle, running from my problems. I'll be home this spring fighting the same demons I fought two weeks ago. Jonah glanced up at Memphis.

Sitting on the prow, Memphis had abandoned his shirt. His tan muscles bounced the sunlight right back into the sky while his blond hair seemed to soak it all in. Barefoot, he dragged his feet in the water from time to time, motioning occasionally with his hands to direct Alejo away from hidden debris. His head swayed back and forth as though a constant and pleasant song played in his head. No bugs bothered him, the heat didn't affect him, and the rushing river only seemed to calm him even more.

Memphis was carefree. No...more than that, he was peaceful, at home with himself. He was serenity personified. He reminds me of someone...but who? Jonah wondered.

"I'll give you a *sol* for your thoughts," Abigail said, offering a small Peruvian coin to Jonah.

Jonah took his eyes off Memphis and tried to push back the thoughts in his head.

"Just trying to take it all in," he said nonchalantly, sitting up and fighting to keep eye contact with Abigail rather than allowing his gaze to drift over to the gorgeous Grace sitting next to her.

"It's beautiful here, isn't it?" Abigail asked.

"Oh yeah. It's great," Jonah said.

"Take it all in while it's new to you. After a while, you sort of get used to the jungle and you forget what a blessing it is to be out in this amazing spot of God's creation without the clutter of buildings and crowds and traffic."

Abigail paused as she slowly rotated her head from side to side, marveling at her environment.

"I think it's absolutely incredible," added Grace.

Suddenly the conversation became more interesting to Jonah.

"Have you ever photographed places like this?" Jonah asked.

"Similar, I suppose, but this river, this jungle, have many unique features that set them apart from any other place in the world."

"Like what?" Jonah asked.

Grace turned her full body toward Jonah, using her hands to point out all of which she spoke.

"Like the intoxicating smells a gentle breeze here can carry," she began. "Like the limitless sky that shows you all it has to offer a million different ways. Like the sounds the birds make just beyond those trees over there, the mystery of the footprints on the beaches alongside the river, and the way the butterflies, with their never-before-seen colors, seem to have come from another world."

Jonah leaned in, instinctively drawn to the poetry that fell from Grace's lips like refreshing drops of water flowing from a cool mountain spring.

"Most of the time, when I travel, I have to create the shot that I want," Grace continued. "I move objects and people around and place them in certain positions in the midst of various photogenic scenes, then I take the picture. Here though, the picture is already created, and it's perfect. My only challenge is how best to capture what is naturally and boldly displayed."

Jonah would have kissed her without a moment of hesitation if there had not been so many strangers present. Instead, he simply nodded his head as if to say, "You stole the words right out of my mouth."

"A jungle is a jungle if you ask me," Basil chimed in.

His cynical contribution caught the group by surprise and everyone turned in time to see Basil closing his file folder and stretching. He rubbed his eyes before returning his attention to his work.

"Hey Jonah, have you been drinking enough water?"

Memphis had come down from the prow of the boat and was now sitting under the roof, in front of Jonah.

"You can get dehydrated pretty fast out here if you're not careful," Memphis said.

Memphis drank a quarter of a liter of water out of an old water bottle, then handed the bottle to Jonah.

"Whoa, what is that taste?" Jonah asked, wiping water from his lips. His grimace gave his opinion away.

"Oh, sorry," Memphis said. "I should've warned you. It's just that, I've become so used to it that I don't even notice it anymore."

"What is it?" Jonah asked.

"Well, that's purified water. Purified with choloraquine pills. It'll kill most of the germs, but it does leave a nasty aftertaste."

Jonah politely handed the water bottle back to Memphis.

"You'll need more than just a few sips to stay hydrated," Memphis said as he finished off the bottle.

"I'll drink some more later," Jonah offered.

Memphis filled the bottle up with river water. Sitting back on the prow of the boat, he resumed his navigation responsibilities while filtering and purifying another liter of water.

Jonah tried to find a comfortable position in his seat. He glanced in Grace's direction, noticing that she had unpacked her camera and was already working on her magazine layout. After a few minutes of staring, Jonah's interest in the Spanish beauty intensified. She was well spoken, intelligent, and now, creative. Without even seeing the images she was capturing, Jonah could discern her talent. What she didn't photograph was just as important as what she did.

Grace skipped over the predictable, computer-screensaver shots, refusing to become a cliché. Instead of the parrot, she captured the colorful flurry of the bird's wing just before it landed on the edge of the boat. Rather than focusing her shots on the dense foliage on the other side of the riverbank, Grace singled out the lone dead tree in the midst of jungle life before snapping the unconventional landscape. Grace prided herself in discovering enigmatic treasures. Capturing unexpected moments in unexpected places, Grace had an eye for what others might overlook.

She turned and caught Jonah watching her. Definitely not a cliché, she thought to herself. Hidden treasure? Perhaps. Grace took his picture.

CHAPTER 18

*T*HE lesser heat that accompanied the gradually setting sun was welcomed by the entire boat party. Memphis slipped his T-shirt back over his head. Jonah looked down at his arms, noticing an obvious sunburn from the first day. Grace finished her first memory card with a shot of Basil sleeping, while Abigail talked in the back of the boat with Alejo and Noah.

"Alejo said we're going to round one more bend before stopping for the night," Abigail called out to the rest of the group.

Jonah sat up at full attention. The thought of going to sleep could not have pleased him more. Memphis grabbed the rope from beneath the prow in preparation to tie up the boat once they stopped.

With the sun now racing to the horizon, Alejo intently looked for a decent beach where the group could pass the night. There was not much daylight left for setting up camp. A lifetime of sleeping on jungle riverbanks afforded Alejo an extremely low standard concerning suitable beaches. Any elevated spot of sand would do.

Noah decreased the speed of the motor by turning a small screw counterclockwise as Alejo had taught him. Traveling against the current, the boat slowly edged up to the riverbank. Alejo turned the motor off and guided the boat near a large trunk that was sticking out of the sand beach. Memphis hurled the rope from the prow of the boat onto the bank, and tied the rope to the protruding tree trunk.

One by one, Grace, Basil, Jonah, and Abigail disembarked with their backpacks while Alejo procured Noah's aid in preparing the boat for its overnight dock. On the beach, Abigail efficiently set up a tent for her and Memphis as she had done a thousand times before. Grace also threw her tent together quickly, as did Basil. Meanwhile, Memphis hunted for dry wood to build a fire for cooking, warmth, and warding off mosquitoes.

Jonah proceeded to tackle the job of setting up a tent for himself and his brother. Their tent, along with the rest of their jungle gear, had been purchased a mere week prior to the trip and still boasted price tags. Jonah had gone camping once when he was nine years old, just before quitting Boy Scouts, but couldn't seem to remember the skills that earned him his camping merit badge. The poles either wouldn't bend or bent too much, the wind kept the tent blowing all over the beach, and more than once the zipper of the tent door hooked itself to Jonah's front pant zipper. Twenty minutes after the other tents were properly assembled, Jonah sat in the middle of a pile of nylon and poles, reading the instruction manual with his headlamp.

"So, how did things turn out with the Amarakaeri?" Basil asked Memphis with a tone of sincere interest rather than the animosity he had shown earlier.

The two men, accompanied by Alejo, Grace, and Abigail, sat by the fire that Memphis had built. In the background, Noah finally came to Jonah's assistance with the tent.

"By the time we left, they were family," Memphis kindly replied. Basil's brief sincerity had proven refreshing.

"I never did understand why they let you stay while forcing me to go," Basil said.

Abigail gave Memphis a knowing look as if to discourage his natural sarcastic nature. Grace and Alejo leaned in, curious about the background of the apparent rivalry between the two men.

"Maybe they perceived, from our part, a genuine interest in their lives," Memphis carefully proposed.

"And from my part?" Basil asked.

"Perhaps, a vague, distanced intrigue."

"I was distanced," Basil agreed. "But for good reason. I didn't wish to interfere with or influence their culture. I simply wanted to observe, to learn about their way of life."

"I think that's commendable," Memphis said. "It is not my desire to change the indigenous people of this country either."

"What do you mean? Your main goal is to try to change the way they are."

"No, not change them. Just give them what we believe to be true. We're mere messengers."

"Western religion should not be imposed on the natives of this jungle."

"It's not a Western religion. And we don't impose it on anyone. There were many families among the Amarakaeri that did not believe the message we brought. We didn't try to force them to change their minds, and we still counted them as friends."

"Look Memphis, in the end, whether you admit it or not, teaching outside beliefs – spiritual or otherwise – will change their tribal culture."

. "He actually seems to have a pretty good point," Noah said as he and Jonah joined the group of travelers around the fire.

Jonah sat down in an empty spot on the same log as Grace. He wiped the sweat from his forehead onto his shirtsleeve.

"Well, thank you, Noah, for your support," Basil said with a smile.

"However, in all fairness, I would also say that even you going there to observe will most likely change their worldview," Noah added. "For an indigenous man or woman who knows nothing but this jungle to see an outsider will inevitably change the way he or she sees and understands this world."

Such a possibility paused the conversation for a moment as each of them considered Noah's comment.

"So then, do you think it's wrong for us to travel all this way to make contact with the Isconahua?" Grace put the question to the entire group.

"I don't think it's wrong, personally, but I think we shouldn't be blind to the consequences such a visit will have on the Isconahua." Noah said.

"I agree with Noah," Memphis said. "Any exposure to the outside world will bring, at the least, a little change. And yet, I believe that the potential benefits that both sides could receive outweigh the risk."

"I don't think our presence alone will prove consequential to their worldview," Basil said. "If we will simply learn their culture without trying to teach them our way of life or religion," he shot a quick glare toward Memphis, "then we can walk away richer and they can remain the same."

Grace pondered Basil's last statement, turning it over in her mind.

"So then, are we just using them?" she asked.

"Using them?" Basil echoed, not understanding.

"You said we would leave richer, having profited by all we learned and observed and experienced – but in what way have they benefited from exposure to us?"

"Interesting observation," Abigail said, obviously in agreement.

"It's that very thing, I think, that kept us in Duba and you out, Basil," added Memphis, eyeing Basil steadily. "We brought them a message of hope and forgiveness and grace and salvation, while you just brought your camera and tape recorder."

Abigail squeezed Memphis's hand. She had seen these two men engage in many heated arguments in the past, and was not prepared to stay up this late at night to see another battle through to the end.

"I think you've made it very clear to us all your opinion of me and my work," Basil said.

"Not you, personally, just the concept of using the indigenous people for our own profit and gain."

Basil shook his head with a smirk that fronted a confidence in the supremacy of his line of thinking over that of Memphis's.

"Some people," Basil began as he looked over each of the faces glowing with light from the dying campfire, "are simply stubborn." He shook his head once more and then walked barefoot across the sand to his one-man tent.

"You two have quite a history, huh?" Jonah inquired of Memphis.

Looking over at Basil's tent, Memphis nodded. For a minute, Memphis was silent.

"If you stay up much longer, you'll want to throw another log on the fire," Memphis finally said, rising and taking his wife's hand. They headed for their tent.

Alejo followed suit, bidding a "buenas noches" to the remaining three.

Outside of their tent, Memphis and Abigail sat on the cool sand. Still holding hands, they began to pray together.

"Father, thank you for bringing us this far so quickly," Abigail began. "We know that you are with us and that you are seeking worshippers for yourself throughout the darkest corners of this jungle. Oh that we could be a part of your mission! I ask that you open up the door for us to take the Gospel to the Isconahua. Give us the chance to share life with this new tribe, just as you did with the Amarakaeri. I ask that you give us the chance to share the story of your salvation. Protect us as we go, and, please, Lord, help us reach the harvest."

Memphis agreed in prayer, enjoying the bold faith of his

wife. Then, he thoughtfully added one more prayer request. "Jesus, I also pray for my new friend, Jonah. I'm not sure what he's looking for, but I pray that in his searching, he finds you."

As Memphis led his wife into their tent, he could still hear the voices coming from the campfire.

Only the Frost brothers and Grace remained. The smaller crowd made Jonah feel more intimate with Grace, a strange, welcomed feeling. Noah recognized his little brother's signs of infatuation and attraction and decided to give Jonah a chance.

"Well, I guess I'll see you two in the morning," Noah said with a yawn. He smacked Jonah on the shoulder as he stepped over the log on his way to the newest tent of the lot.

Jonah stared into the fire, suddenly uncomfortable with the situation. It's one thing to admire Grace's unprecedented beauty from afar, but to be the only one in her presence sent his emotions and nerves flipping around inside of him.

"I see you finally got your tent set up," Grace said. Her smile jumped from her face to Jonah's.

"Yeah, I guess I'm not much of an outdoorsman."

"And you are not much of a linguist either?"

"No."

"An anthropologist?"

"No."

"Missionary?"

Jonah laughed. "No."

"Photographer?" Grace held her camera up.

"No," Jonah said.

"Well, then, what are you doing here, Jonah Frost?"

Grace playfully took a picture of Jonah.

Is she flirting with me? Jonah wondered.

"My brother invited me," Jonah said, hoping that would end the interrogation.

"You don't have to work?" Grace pried.

Her straightforward questions didn't bother Jonah much. He was just glad to be talking with her.

"To be honest with you, I sort of got fired about a month ago."

"I'm sorry to hear that. What was your line of work?"

"I was a teacher at a community college in New York City."

"History?"

"No. Creative writing. Why would you assume history?"

"I thought that maybe that was the source of your interest in indigenous cultures."

"Oh, well, I don't really have an interest in indigenous cultures – or the jungle, or even other countries, for that matter. I'm pretty happy in the city. I just came because my brother invited me."

"Sure you did. Noah invited you to come live in the jungle for three months, and, even though you are not the least bit interested in such things, you readily agreed to tag along. Come on, Jonah, what really brought you here?" Grace probed.

Jonah fixed his attention on the flames of the fire. The way the orange danced with the blue and flirted with the red found Jonah in a trance, allowing his mind to flash back undistracted.

One scene followed by others entered his mind, flashing from one to the next like movie clips: There was Jonah in his kitchen, typing a suicide letter to his brother. Jonah sitting in his truck with a bottle of whiskey to help him finish off the first bottle of pain pills. Jonah lay across the truck's front seat, his stomach turning and his truck running, listening to an old song while he waited to die. His brother grabbing his hand from the green chair beside his hospital bed. An older man by the name of Gary trading stories with Jonah at his first AA meeting a week before Christmas.

Jonah, saying nothing, looked back up at Grace.

"What was it, Jonah? What was it that made you want to escape?" Grace leaned in with a sincere expression of concern and interest.

"I used to be a writer, Grace. I used to be thought a brilliant writer with unlimited potential."

Jonah hesitated. How honest should he be with this Spanish photographer he just met? He looked up at the sky. He had never seen so many stars in his life.

"I guess the truth is, Grace, I came out here to find a story worth writing."

Grace smiled, recognizing that she had heard but a portion of the truth. She sensed that there was more to Jonah than even he knew. With time, perhaps they would both discover the man hidden beneath the confusion and uncertainty.

"I hope you find what you're looking for, Jonah." Grace slightly patted Jonah's knee before standing up and leaving for her tent.

Left alone with the fire and his thoughts, Jonah watched the river gently rocking their boat as it flowed past the campsite. For an instant, it gave him an idea for a story. As the words began to form sentences, Jonah shook the thought out of his head.

"Not yet," he said to himself. "Not yet."

CHAPTER 19

A DENSE fog rested on the surface of the river the following morning. Not even an expert motorist could maneuver a boat up the river through such a thick haze. Still, Alejo, again enlisting Noah's help, loaded the boat and filled the gas tank.

Basil brushed his teeth in the river. Memphis filtered water next to the boat. Abigail and Grace searched out a suitable spot to use the bathroom among the bushes near the edge of the forest, and Jonah stood on the sandy beach wondering why he was awake and covered with mosquitoes before the sun was even up.

"Jonah, come drink some of this water." Memphis was wading in the river, holding up a liter of cloudy river water.

Jonah stumbled down the bank's slope toward Memphis. Memphis tossed Jonah the bottle.

"Is it clean?" he asked.

"It's purified, so it won't make you sick," Memphis replied. "But, as you can see, it's not Evian."

"It's brown."

Memphis laughed.

"Get used to it, buddy. It's as clean as you're going to get for the next three months. But it'll keep you alive. You need to drink about three liters a day to stay hydrated in the jungle heat. Your brother already finished a half bottle this morning. Go ahead and finish that liter before we leave, and I'll get you some more later."

Jonah examined the water, and then took a sip. The dirty

water, mixed with the aftertaste of the purification pills Memphis used, did not sit well with Jonah. He immediately spit out the water and promised himself he'd never again drink anything Memphis gave him.

"¿Estás listo?" Alejo asked Jonah.

"Uh, what?"

"You have been ready to go, no?" Alejo tried in his broken English.

"Oh, uh, yeah."

The girls settled into the front bench again and were off talking like old friends once more. Noah assumed his spot as second captain across from Alejo, just behind Basil who was already reviewing papers using his headlamp. Memphis untied the boat and pushed it into the river before jumping onto the prow at the last second, and Jonah, on the left side of the middle bench, sat useless, holding a full liter of cloudy purified water.

The morning fog gradually lifted as Alejo steered his passengers up the Piedras River for their second day in a row.

About an hour into the trip, someone finally acknowledged Jonah.

"Jonah, you never contributed to our little debate last night by the fire," Basil suddenly commented from the back row. "I'd be interested to hear what you think about the extent of our involvement with natives."

"Oh, I really don't have an opinion," Jonah said.

"You know what, Jonah, that's exactly what I thought you would say," Basil said. "You don't seem to have much stake in any of this."

"No, I guess not. I'm just here to share the adventure with my brother."

"He's a writer," Grace added, joining the conversation. "He thinks this journey to another world will give him an idea for a story."

Under other circumstances, Jonah would have been offended by Grace's assuming role as she spoke for him, but in her case, he was just glad they had an opportunity to talk again. He hoped she was, in some way, intrigued by his self-proclaimed aptitude for creativity.

"Is that right?" Basil asked. "A writer? Well, you're bound to find a story out here."

Jonah nodded his head as if that meant something to him.

"I adore writers," Basil continued. "I, for one, carry no aspirations to write. However, I am an avid reader and therefore truly appreciate those who create the books that I read."

"Who's your favorite author?" Jonah asked, relieved to be talking about something he actually understood.

"James Joyce."

"Joyce?"

"The Irish stick together."

Jonah laughed at Basil's qualifications for his favorite author.

"Did you bring any of your previous stories?" Grace asked, turning the conversation back to Jonah's writing rather than that of Joyce.

"No," Jonah answered abruptly.

"Well, you'll have to promise to let me read whatever you write about our little trip here," she said.

"I'll be interested to read it as well," Basil added.

"Deal," Jonah said without conviction.

Grace smiled. Her eyes held a confidence in them, a confidence in Jonah. She looked at him as though she knew that he would indeed write a brilliant story that she would one day read. Jonah searched her eyes further. He smiled. She believed in him.

"Hey, Jonah, why don't you come up here and learn how to be the point man?" Memphis called out from the front of the boat.

The idea of actually contributing something to this trip greatly appealed to Jonah. He politely dismissed himself from his conversation with Grace and Basil and hurried to the front of the boat. Memphis dropped down from the prow and kneeled next to Jonah.

"Basics first," Memphis began. "It's all about reading the river. Everything the river is doing, every different spot you can see, is telling you something. All you have to do is listen with your eyes."

"Listen with your eyes?" Jonah repeated.

"That's right. You see all of those little ripples on the side of the river over there to the left?"

"Yeah."

"Well, the water is rippling like that because it's hitting rocks and rolling over them. That tells us that the water is shallow right there. If Alejo drove over those ripples right now, we'd crash onto the rocks and be stuck."

"Have you ever hit rocks before?" Jonah asked.

"A million times. You have to jump out and push the boat back into the current."

Memphis continued teaching Jonah how to discern the signs of the current and then relate that information back to Alejo. Memphis pointed out eddies and hydraulics and vortexes and even camouflaged alligator heads, which, in Jonah's opinion, were floating too close to the boat. After an hour of instruction, Memphis handed the job over to Jonah and then retired on the bench next to Abigail.

From his seat, Memphis watched Jonah as he prayed inwardly for his new friend to find the kind of life that only Jesus Christ can give.

From the prow of the boat, Jonah began to direct Alejo away from shallow spots and floating debris. Alejo quietly laughed as Jonah overcautiously pointed out every stick and leaf on the course, fearing that all jeopardized the boat.

By afternoon, the Frost brothers were leading the expedition as Noah drove the boat, following Jonah's navigational directions. Who would have thought that two city boys could come down to the Amazon jungle and taxi a bunch of strangers to an unknown tribal people?

Sweltering heat blistered Jonah's shoulders and led the rest of the party to cry for a swim break. Alejo helped Noah carefully dock the boat under the shade of some overhanging trees where Jonah tied his best knot. The ladies dove into the cooling water in their shorts and sports bras, while the men stripped down to their underwear. It was a sweltering and humid 103 degrees. This was not the time for modesty.

Dipping his head back into the water, Jonah felt relief from the heat for the first time in hours. Grace swam as low as she could in order to escape every single sunray, while Memphis and Abigail waded in the shallow waters under the shade of the tree. Basil ate a granola bar and Noah shared some beef jerky with Alejo, who had never tasted dried meat before and was immediately hooked.

"Put in mail for me from los Estados Unidos," he kept saying to Noah.

A little more bold than usual after proving his worth all day as the point man, Jonah swam over to Grace.

"Are you used to this heat yet?" he asked, immediately cursing himself silently for opening with a line about the weather.

"I don't think I'll ever be used to it being this hot all the time," Grace answered. "You seem to be doing fine, though. You make a fine point man."

Ah, so she noticed, Jonah thought to himself.

"Yeah, well, I guess some guys are naturally made for the rough life."

"Apparently so," Grace responded with a giggle.

"The truth is, I'm still pretty much hating the discomfort of it all. There are bugs everywhere, the sun keeps getting hotter, my skin feels blistered, and I am dying of thirst."

"Have you been drinking water today, Jonah?"

Grace seemed truly concerned, and Jonah, suddenly self-conscious, didn't want to appear as if he didn't know how to survive in the wild.

"Of course I've been drinking water. I've had close to three liters today," he lied. "But I'm still thirsty."

"Yeah, me too," Grace acknowledged.

That was close, Jonah thought.

"¿Listo?" Alejo asked. *Ready?*

Everyone swam back to the boat where they put their clothes back on over their wet bodies. Memphis resumed point, allowing Jonah a break in the shade, and Alejo took over the driving responsibilities. Noah moved to the bench next to Jonah where the two brothers invented games in order to pass the last few hours on the river.

CHAPTER 20

SEVERAL hours later, on another beach further up the Piedras River, the crew quickly set up camp in a race against the setting sun. Memphis came to Jonah's rescue when he became tangled in the tent and tent poles, and together they were able to assemble the tent before the last light of day faded into darkness. Tired, sunburned, worn out, and covered with itching bug bites, the entire group zipped themselves into their tents, forgoing the campfire debriefing.

With his arm under Abigail's head, Memphis stared up at the stars illuminating the jungle night. He tried to imagine Artone, rivers away, staring at the same constellations that filled the small net window making up the roof of Memphis's tent. Reminiscing about former hunting trips with his good friend brought a grin to Memphis's face and a tear to his eye.

"Budteré," he softly said, not wanting to forget his Duba name. When would he ever again be known as Budteré?

With reason to praise fresh on his mind, Memphis quietly sang his favorite hymn, the hymn that often came to mind as he waited for sleep to overtake him.

> *Be Thou my Vision, O Lord of my heart.*
> *Nought be all else to me, save that Thou art.*
> *Thou my best thought, by day or by night.*
> *Waking or sleeping, Thy presence my light.*

Abigail turned in her sleep and Memphis closed his eyes in an effort to join her.

Basil lay motionless less than ten yards from the Jones' tent.

His loud and obnoxious snoring, coupled with his heavy and deep breathing, rivaled the other noises of the rainforest. Echoes of monkey cries and frog calls and songs sung by passing parrots seemed to fade as Basil's snoring drowned out all other sounds.

Fortunately for Alejo, Basil's closest neighbor on the beach, the snoring was no match for the exhaustion that could only be known by a motorist. Alejo had driven a loaded boat upriver against a strong current for more than ten hours for the second day in a row. He slept deeply.

Lying next to his brother, Jonah fought the gradually increasing pain in his side. Fifteen minutes before, he had thought it to be nothing more than an indication of his need to use the bathroom, but after trekking outside his tent and into the jungle, he returned unable to go and hurting all the more. He now racked his brain as to what the cause of the pain could be.

At first it felt like a side cramp. But the cramp grew to a feeling of constipation, which gave way to a slight stinging before climaxing into a full-grown sensation of a sharp pain like knives piercing his ribcage. Jonah squinted his eyes as he grimaced in pain. Not wanting to wake up Noah, he unzipped the tent and walked over to the spot of the dwindling fire.

Jonah let out a restrained yell, gripping his right side with his hand. The pain shot through his nerves like porcupine needles under his skin. The pain dropped Jonah to his knees in the cold sand where he looked up to the sky and cried out in agony before falling onto his back.

As he gripped his side more tightly, the sharp pain seemed to be gravitating to a lower part of his side. Jonah beat his fist onto the ground, rolling around on the beach as sand filled his every crevice.

"Jonah? What's wrong?" a worried voice called out from somewhere behind him.

Jonah leaned his head back to determine the face behind the voice, while continuing to roll back and forth in the sand. To his embarrassment, he realized it was Grace, no doubt awakened from her sleep by his cries of pain.

"Are you sick?" she asked as she approached him.

"I don't know," Jonah managed to get out through tightly closed lips. "My side is killing me."

Grace knelt down in the sand next to Jonah. Using her left hand to hold him still, she felt along his side with her right hand. Noticing no swelling, she carefully observed Jonah.

"Jonah, does it feel like a sharp pain?" she asked.

"Yes."

"Does the pain seem to be moving at all?"

"A little. It's going lower in my side."

Jonah rolled away from Grace. Suddenly he jumped up and ran toward a pile of sticks and logs a few feet away. He bent forward and began vomiting violently.

"I'll be right back," Grace said, apparently unaffected by the disgusting nature of what she had just witnessed.

Jonah continued to throw up everything that was in him. Grace returned with a liter of water and two pills to calm the stomach.

"Jonah, did you really drink three liters of water today?" she asked as he wiped some repulsive yellow substance off the corner of his mouth with the back of his hand.

He thought about Grace's question and then remembered the cloudy bottle of gross water Memphis had given him early that morning. The full bottle remained stashed under his bench on the boat. Jonah shook his head "no" in response to Grace's inquiry.

"I think you have a kidney stone," Grace said. "You're dehydrated, and unless we get some water in you, you're going to become extremely sick."

Grace handed Jonah the pills and water.

"Take these pills to calm your stomach so that you won't just throw up all the water you drink. And drink this entire bottle of water. Hopefully, we can hydrate you so you don't get sick. As far as the kidney stone goes, though, you're just going to have to wait it out and pass it."

Jonah swallowed the pills, washing them down with his first good drink of water in more than twenty-four hours.

"So this pain isn't going to stop?" Jonah asked, squeezing his side now with both hands.

"It'll probably hurt until the stone passes into your bladder," Grace said. "Have you ever had a kidney stone before?"

Jonah shook his head. The pain brought him to his knees again.

"Well, you've got a little ball of spikes the size of a grain of sand moving through your body right now. I know it hurts, but it won't last much longer."

Jonah rolled on the ground, not comforted by Grace's words.

"Don't worry, Jonah, I'll be right here with you as long as you're in pain," Grace said, taking hold of Jonah's free hand.

Immediately, he began to feel better.

The anguish of a traveling kidney stone plagued Jonah for two and a half hours as Grace stayed faithfully by his side, keeping him hydrated and comforted. The two returned to their respective tents around three in the morning, after Jonah's pain finally subsided. An hour and a half later, they were awakened to begin packing up their tents and backpacks for another long day on the river.

"Did you pass it?"

Jonah was urinating behind two trees when Grace shouted at him from the beach.

"Did you pass the stone?" she repeated.

"I don't know. How can you tell?"

"It looks like a tiny rock or a grain of sand. See anything?"

"We're on a beach, Grace. Everything I'm peeing on looks like grains of sand."

Grace laughed.

"Maybe you've just passed about a thousand kidney stones," she said.

"Maybe." Jonah finished and began walking toward Grace. "Either way, I feel a million times better."

"I'm glad," Grace said, touching Jonah's shoulder. "Are you going to actually drink water today?"

"You bet. I don't care how brown it is or how gross it tastes, if it'll keep me from having to go through that again, then it's worth it."

Grace nodded in agreement as the two walked side by side to the boat where the rest of the group finished loading the gear.

"Hey, thanks for staying up with me last night," Jonah said.

"You're welcome," Grace replied with a smile. "We'll have to do it again sometime."

"Deal."

"And maybe next time, I won't have to watch you throw up all over yourself," Grace winked at Jonah before stepping into the boat.

CHAPTER 21

*F*OLLOWING two full days of river travel, exhaustion infused the group of foreigners hoping to be the first outsiders accepted by the Isconahua.

Alejo, though an experienced motorist, began to feel the first stages of fatigue. His arms were sore from maneuvering the weighted boat through the narrow river full of sharp bends and floating debris. By his calculations, and in accordance with the reports of the Isconahua village that was discovered, Alejo determined they would need three more full days before they reached the Angosto River. From there, the group would require another two days up an even narrower river before arriving at the Isconahuas' village. The sheer thought of the length of the trip that lay ahead of him made his muscles all the more weary.

If only we had fewer people, he thought, we'd be able to cut off an entire day of travel. If only they were paying me more. Perhaps then it'd be worth the trip.

While religiously drinking a liter of muddy, yet purified, water, Jonah sat on the front seat of the boat, relaying to Noah the story of his kidney stone and the unbearable pain of the night before. He was careful to include every detail about Grace and how she stayed awake with him throughout the long night. Two rows behind the Frost brothers, Abigail received the same story from Grace. Grace even described the disgusting vomit attacks she witnessed.

"So, do you think there's something there?" Abigail asked. "I mean, between you and Jonah?"

"Oh, no, I don't think so," Grace replied. "He's good looking and interesting and all, but, well, I just don't think he even knows himself yet. It's hard to truly get to know somebody like that."

"He does seem a bit lost," Abigail affirmed. "It's like he's spent his life searching for some sort of hidden treasure and then suddenly realized he had the wrong map. Now he has nothing but pain to show for his journey."

"Well, what about you? What, exactly, are you looking to get out of this journey?" Grace asked. "I know that you're a missionary, but what does that actually involve?"

Abigail took time to think of her response.

"That's a great question," she said. "In fact, if you ask a hundred different missionaries that same question, you'll probably get about a hundred different answers. For me, though, all I want to get from this journey is the chance to tell people about the love of my life."

"I assume you didn't come all this way to tell some naked tribesmen about Memphis, so…who is this love of your life?"

Like Grace with her photography, Abigail worked hard to avoid evangelistic clichés. She drank some water, allowing the conversational recess to take her back to the beginning of her story. Grace patiently waited.

"When I was sixteen years old, my dad left my mom," Abigail said. "He left her for a younger, prettier woman. I only saw her once, but I could clearly see that she was gorgeous. At first, I hated him for leaving us, but then soon after I saw his new girlfriend, I began to resent my mother."

"Why? What had she done?"

"Nothing. I know that now, of course, but then, I thought that she had failed to keep her husband. In my adolescent mind, it was her fault because she hadn't made herself pretty enough to keep him. I was determined to be nothing like her. Looking back, I think I was trying to make sure that in my own relationships, I would not be my mom, I'd be the prettier, more desirable woman.

"Long story short, I developed a bunch of problems ranging from anorexia to depression. Eventually, the depression ran so deep that I could feel it."

"You felt sad?"

"No, it was more than that, and deeper than that – I felt the depression itself. It was palpable, as if I was walking around with a heavy sack over my shoulder that was filled with every negative emotion that I had ever experienced. It affected every area of my life. Then, years later, through a series of long conversations with my college freshman roommate, I discovered that Jesus Christ has the power to take that bag off my shoulder forever. I could, in effect, trade my despair for His peace. I trusted him with my many problems and He set me free. Only then could I become the woman He created me to be. In that, He became the love of my life."

Grace smiled and reached over to give Abigail a hug.

"Thanks for sharing your story with me," Grace said. "I needed to hear that. You know, I guess everyone needs to hear it. I don't know much about missionaries or whether or not Basil has a point about us introducing new ideas to the indigenous, but I suspect even the Isconahua need to hear how God can change a person's life."

The two women leaned back in their chairs, appreciating a brief gust of wind that momentarily cooled their faces. Behind them, Basil kept Alejo company while Memphis again served as point man at the front of the boat.

Without warning, the speed of the boat slowed considerably. Suddenly, Alejo steered the oversize canoe to the left bank of the river. Memphis assumed their driver needed to either fill up the gas tank or empty his bladder, so he jumped onto the muddy beach with the rope in hand. He glanced back at their motorist to figure out the purpose of the stop.

"Barbasco!" Alejo shouted. "Many barbasco," he said, trying to help out his English speakers.

Jonah, Noah, and Grace just stared at the man who splashed water into the boat as he jumped out and ran up the riverbank with his machete.

"What's wrong?" Jonah asked with a bit of fear vibrating in his voice. He suddenly wished he had a machete and knew how to use it.

"Everything's fine," Memphis said, tying the rope to a stable log. "Our friend, with his keen eye, apparently spotted some barbasco on this bank."

"What does that mean?" Jonah asked.

"It means we're going fishing," Basil translated as he too disembarked from the boat and headed up the beach to help Alejo.

"Barbasco is a root," Abigail began to explain. "The locals here pull it out of the ground, break it up with rocks, and then use it to fish. When you shake it in the water, it releases a white, milky substance that partially paralyzes the fish."

"The fish just float to the top of the water?" Noah asked.

"Some will be that easy to catch," Abigail answered. "But the big fish will become a bit disoriented. They'll still be moving and flopping around, but they'll be closer to the surface of the water. That's when you spear them."

"Spear them?" Jonah asked, suddenly wishing he had a spear and knew how to use it.

"That's right. Spear them," Abigail repeated. "Don't worry, Memphis will teach you."

She grabbed a machete and exited the boat.

"Come on," she called out to the inexperienced Frost brothers. "First we've got to get the barbasco."

Without a machete to spare, the diverse group of seven spread out across a field of plants that Alejo had identified as barbasco. The men cut the ground loose around the small plants before completely pulling them out of the earth. The two ladies began cutting the roots off each plant.

"You stupid, stubborn...."

"Here, let me help," Memphis interrupted.

Jonah had been struggling with one of the larger plants while Memphis and the other men had yanked them out one after another like a dentist with a firm grip on a loose tooth. He had finally resorted to cursing the shrub in an effort to force it out of the ground.

"You sure did pick a big one," Memphis said.

Jonah immediately felt better about his inability to remove the thing.

"I guess I needed a challenge," he said.

Comfortable with his machete as if it were an extension of his hand, Memphis swiftly and efficiently cut a circle in the ground around the plant, loosening the dirt considerably.

"Now, Jonah, you just grab it on the trunk like this, and push it as hard as you can back and forth," he said. "Just sort of shake it loose."

Jonah took hold of the wide trunk and began to pull and then push with all of his strength. For a man who had not even thought about working out since high school, Jonah found a surprising amount of muscle in his arms. The leaves fell and some of the smaller branches broke as Jonah shook the barbasco plant violently. This was a battle, a battle Jonah refused to lose.

His arms flexed as an unusual amount of sweat poured from his forehead and under his arms. Jonah hadn't exerted this much physical energy in years. Gradually, the firm plant began to yield.

"Ahhhh!" Jonah shouted as he tore it from the ground, falling backwards onto the beach, the plant landing on top of him. By this point, everyone was watching.

"That's what I'm talking about!" Memphis shouted. "You're the man, Jonah! You are the man!"

Memphis effortlessly tossed the plant off Jonah, grabbed his hand, and pulled him to his feet. Jonah wiped some dirt off his hands the way he had once seen a working man do it on TV.

"Nice work, buddy," Memphis said.

He didn't know why, but, for some reason, to hear Memphis not only compliment him but call him "buddy" gave Jonah a greater sense of self-affirmation than he had felt in many years.

"That was impressive," Grace added, walking over to the hero of the moment. Without hesitating, she reached out to wipe sweat off Jonah's forehead. She glanced over at the barbasco roots hanging from the large bush he had uprooted. "Well, this ought to catch us some fish."

Grace joined Abigail and began chopping the roots with her machete.

After two hours of gathering barbasco, the hopeful anglers

boasted enough to have filled a dozen baskets with the root. They distributed the weight evenly throughout the boat when they returned. Alejo filled the gas tank while Basil relieved himself on the beach. Once everyone had taken their seats, Memphis untied the rope and pushed the boat away from the bank. Alejo started the peke-peke motor and the travelers were on their way toward the Isconahua once more.

"Alejo said we'll stop and fish once we find a canal," Memphis announced.

CHAPTER 22

THE hours following the group's morning of gathering barbasco ushered in an unbearably hot afternoon. The sun's rays penetrated even the roof of the boat and heated every atom of oxygen so that the air itself was difficult to inhale. The crew of seven worked hard to stay cool.

Abigail taught Grace the trick of soaking a T-shirt in the river and then wearing it has a bonnet, allowing the water to pour and then drip all over her. Memphis dragged his feet in the water as he continued to direct Alejo from the prow of the boat. Jonah chugged liter after liter of purified river water as Noah followed suit, heeding the warning of Jonah's dehydration-induced kidney stone. At the back of the boat, Basil attempted to lower his body temperature with a fan he frantically waved next to his face. Alejo merely kept his head wet, pausing periodically to dunk it over the side of the boat into the cooling water.

The heat had stopped all conversation. Memphis noticed that the group needed something to distract them from their burnt shoulders, pouring sweat, and weary spirits. He was about to suggest a swim break when he spotted a canal just before the next bend.

"Alejo, hay un quebrada un poco mas adelante," he shouted. *Alejo, there is a canal just a bit further ahead.*

Alejo stood and saw the canal. He looked at Memphis and nodded.

"Vamos a pescar," *Let's go fishing,* said Alejo, momentarily forgetting the Frost brothers' lack of Spanish. "Fish," he said to Jonah and Noah, pointing ahead.

The idea of abandoning the boat to immerse themselves in the river appealed to all and instantly the mood of the group lightened.

Upon arriving at the entrance of the canal, Alejo decreased the velocity of the boat dramatically until the boat was barely moving. Memphis moved to the back of the boat where he and Alejo formulated a plan for the fishing detour. Memphis and Basil then began to gather the necessary tools: three spears, two baskets, two machetes, and a large net.

"Jonah, why don't you come with us?" Memphis said before following Basil with a leap from the boat onto the muddy ground surrounding the shallow waters of the narrow canal.

Jonah smiled and picked up a machete.

Alejo, Noah, Abigail, and Grace left the three men at the mouth of the channel, as Alejo brilliantly maneuvered the boat through the first hairpin turn.

"So what's the plan?" Jonah asked.

Basil was already cutting down long bamboo stalks.

"You and I are going to help Basil set up the net," Memphis explained. "Once the net is in place, we'll wait here while the rest of the group breaks up the barbasco and shakes it in the water upriver, releasing the magic liquid." Memphis smiled at his own description.

"Then we spear them," Jonah said, quoting Abigail from earlier.

"That's right. We three will bring in the larger fish while the other four row back toward us, scooping up the fish in baskets and spearing the ones that get stuck on the sides of the bank. The net will catch any that get past us."

"How long will it take Alejo to travel up the canal?" Jonah asked.

"About fifteen minutes. Then, they'll spend another twenty minutes preparing the roots. It'll be forty minutes or so before the fish down here are affected. But once the barbasco juice reaches us, we'd better be ready with the net."

Basil returned with four long bamboo poles.

"These should suffice," he said.

Following Memphis's directions, Jonah and Basil spread the net across the entrance of the canal, Jonah grabbing one end of the net and swimming to the other side of the canal while Basil held the other end taut. The channel was narrow and the current weak, so spreading the net took little effort from the two men.

Meanwhile Memphis grabbed two of the bamboo poles and waded into the water. He pushed the first one through the holes of the side of the net that Basil held, digging it into the mud so that it stood straight. Swimming to the other side of the canal, Memphis repeated the same with Jonah's end.

Basil tossed Memphis another pole that he wove through a section of the net between Jonah's side and the middle of the canal. In order to bury this one into the bottom of the river, he had to hold his breath and work underwater. He surfaced a minute or so later with the job complete. One more tossed pole from Basil and one more underwater dig on Memphis's part, and the net was in place. The bottom of the net reached all the way to the river bottom and left little room for fish to escape.

Memphis handed Jonah a spear and told him to stay on his side of the canal. He then swam back to where Basil waited on the bank with two spears. Basil handed one of the spears to Memphis as he stepped out of the river. In the distance, the men could hear Alejo turning off the motor.

"I guess they made it," Memphis assumed. "Another twenty-five minutes or so and we'll be ready to fish. Jonah, put your spear into any fish you can reach over there, and Basil and I will take care of this side."

Given their history and obvious dislike for one another, Jonah was surprised by the unity with which Memphis and Basil seemed to work. However, it had been his experience that, in the case of men, even the greatest of enemies can get along if they're fishing.

"How many times have you fished with burbisco?" Jonah asked the other men, mispronouncing the name of the plant.

"It's barbasco," Basil corrected.

"Oh, right. Barbasco," Jonah repeated.

"Some locals taught me more than a decade ago," Basil said. "Since then, I've probably been fishing more times with barbasco than without it."

"What's the largest catch you've ever had using this stuff?" Jonah asked.

"Well, I cannot recall precisely. Perhaps, three hundred."

"Three hundred fish!" Jonah exclaimed.

"That's correct. And you, Memphis?" Basil asked.

"I guess we've filled about nine baskets before," Memphis answered. "So, I guess, around two hundred or so."

"You fished with the Amarakaeri in Duba?" Basil asked for clarification.

"Yeah, especially with Art. He and I used to row to a quiet little lagoon and fish with our bows and arrows from the canoe. We wouldn't use barbasco then, though."

"Who exactly is Art?" Basil inquired.

"Well, his real name is Artone. We just called him Art."

"I see," Basil said with a head nod and more than a little frustration. "So, Memphis, you fished with the Amarakaeri. You lived with them. And, now you are informing me that you gave them English nicknames?"

"We also hunted and cooked and sang and laughed and prayed and wept and worked with them," Memphis added. "But we didn't give them all nicknames. Just Art and Jenny, our closest friends. You know, they gave me a nickname, too."

Basil shook his head and walked across the muddy bank closer to Memphis.

"This is my first time to fish in the jungle," Jonah quickly called out from the opposite bank, trying to derail the tense conversation slowly building between the other men. No one seemed to hear him, though.

"It is apparent, Memphis, that you find it amusing that the Duba people failed to welcome me, an educated man with interests to merely learn from the culture without altering their way of life, while accepting you, an American Christian with the sole intent of changing their beliefs and values in accordance with your Western religion," Basil said, maintaining eye contact with Memphis the entire time. "I, on the other hand, can think of nothing else less amusing and more tragic than what you and your obnoxious little wife have done to the Amarakaeri people group."

"Be careful, Basil," Memphis interjected. "You've made your opinions of my involvement with any indigenous group quite clear, and you're free to do so again, no matter how misinformed your opinions are. However, you are not free to insult my wife."

Memphis's voice was firm, his face tense, and even his muscles seemed to protrude involuntarily as he spoke.

"You ruin their culture, and all you hear is one little comment about your wife. Oh, how dense you must be!"

"We didn't ruin anything. We didn't even change anything. We simply shared our beliefs about Jesus Christ with them and then left it to them to decide whether or not it was a truth they desired to follow."

"Of course they are going to follow what you teach. They are uneducated, wild savages who are easily influenced by anything a white foreigner might say. The ignorant will always find wisdom in that of which they know nothing."

Memphis gripped his spear tighter and inched closer to Basil's beard. Jonah watched painfully from the other side of the canal, unsure whether or not he should intervene.

"Basil, you obstinate, cold-hearted, arrogant man," Memphis began. "The Duba people are not savages. They are not ignorant or even uneducated. As you said, it was people like them who taught you how to fish. They know who they are. They know the jungle in which they live, and they are perfectly capable of deciding whether or not to believe what we teach."

"You manipulated them," Basil said with a raised voice. "And you are planning to manipulate the Isconahua as well, and I will not allow it."

"You won't allow it?" Memphis shouted sarcastically. "Basil Cosgrove, my wife and I are going to live with the Isconahua and share our lives and the Gospel with them as we did with the Amarakaeri, and there is nothing you can do to stop us!"

The men were now chest to chest, employing the full thrust of their lungs as they yelled back and forth at one another.

"I will expose you!" Basil shouted.

"Expose what? We're missionaries! It's no secret. It's you and your view of the natives out here that needs to be exposed."

"You're going to build another 'little America' in their village," Basil said disdainfully.

"And you're going to sit back and observe your 'savages,' watching them like animals in cages at your own personal zoo," Memphis shot back with equal disdain.

"I will not allow you to ruin my work again!"

"Don't worry, they're going to kick you out just as they kicked you out of Duba."

"Memphis, I hope they kill you and abuse your wife as the village slave!"

At this, Memphis quickly punched him in the jaw causing Basil to drop his spear and fall backward into the mud.

"Memphis, don't!" Jonah shouted, jumping in the water to swim to the fight.

Basil slid the back of his left hand across the red mark Memphis's punch left on his jaw.

"What kind of Christian hits a man?" Basil shouted. "I knew that you and that tramp of yours were imposters."

"That's enough!" Memphis exploded with rage, his tan face burning red. In one rapid motion, Memphis gripped his spear with both hands, his knuckles white, lifted it in the air and violently plunged it down toward Basil's neck as if he were another jaguar to be killed. Without enough time to react in any other way, Basil's reflexes merely enabled him to squint his eyes at the coming blow.

"Memphis!" A woman's scream echoed through the jungle from the approaching boat.

Before the spear could pierce Basil's skin, Jonah lunged from the water and threw himself against Memphis, tackling him to the ground. The three men lay spread out on the bank, each trying to catch his breath. Fifteen yards away, a stunned Abigail stared at her husband, her mouth and eyes wide open. Alejo and Noah continued to row toward the unbelievable scene.

"Lunatic!" Basil hollered at Memphis. "You were going to kill me! Is that in your Bible? Is that what you teach the natives? Is that what being a missionary is all about? Is that what Christians do? Kill people?"

Basil slowly rose to his feet, brushing himself off.

"Abigail, will you please tell me more about your God?" He called out, sarcastically. "I want to be saved so that I can go around killing people with spears."

Alejo and Noah helped Basil back into the boat. He was still shaking from the sight of the point of Memphis's approaching spear in what he thought would be his last moment on earth.

Abigail ignored his mocking plea for salvation and ran over to Memphis while Grace headed toward Jonah.

Memphis sat up and Abigail fell to her knees on the beach to cradle his head and chest in her arms.

"What happened?" she pleaded with her husband.

"I don't know," he said, his breath and senses reluctantly returning to him. Memphis looked around in disbelief and then back at Abigail. "We were arguing, and he said something terrible about you, and then…I just lost it."

Grace helped Jonah find sure footing in the muddy bank. Jonah's heart had not stopped racing. His nerves were ragged.

"Are you alright?" Grace asked, concern resonating in her voice.

"I think so," Jonah said. "I don't know what happened."

"You saved Basil's life," she said. "That's what happened."

CHAPTER 23

MEMPHIS'S attack on Basil brought the fishing expedition to an abrupt halt. Noah and Alejo retrieved the net and poles, gathering four baskets of fish from the surface of the water as they worked. Abigail sat next to Memphis in the boat, holding his hand. Behind them, Grace and Jonah sat closer than ever, stunned by what they had just witnessed. Basil sat alone, making meaningless notes and fuming.

Following the fishing trip and a pit stop, the group was left with only two hours of daylight. Alejo navigated another hour and a half before stopping at a beach where they would rest for the night. Quietly and mechanically, everyone unloaded their gear, set up their tents, and turned in without a word.

Jonah gave Grace one of those awkward hugs men give women they like when they're not sure if the woman likes them too. She confidently squeezed Jonah back.

"I'll see you in the morning," Jonah whispered.

"Good night, Jonah," Grace whispered back.

He loved hearing her say his name.

In his tent, Jonah settled into his sleeping bag.

"How are you doing, little brother?" Noah asked.

"Not bad. I'm still in a bit of shock, though."

"I think we all are. I can't believe Memphis attacked Basil like that. If it weren't for you, he would have killed him. You were brave today, Jonah."

"It was all such a blur. I didn't even know what I was doing. I don't know, though, if Memphis would have really killed him."

"Are you kidding me? He was an inch away from his neck with that spear. What happened anyway?"

"Basil and Memphis were arguing about whether or not the other one should enter the Isconahua village. They were insulting each other, yelling about how the other one was going to ruin everything and how they didn't belong there. Then, Basil said something about Abigail being used by the villagers as a whore, and I guess that just set Memphis off. He punched Basil and then lifted his spear to stab him. He really just lost it, you know?"

Noah stared up at the stars, processing the story.

"I guess if someone called my wife a tramp, I'd hit him too," he said. "I don't think I'd kill him, though. Maybe all his time in the jungle, you know, running around hunting wild animals and living with the natives and all, has sort of changed Memphis into...."

"Into what?" Jonah asked.

"I don't know. Maybe, uncivilized."

Jonah nodded in silent agreement.

"Maybe so."

On the other side of the beach, Memphis lay wide-awake with Abigail's head resting on his bare chest.

"You've always defended me, Memphis," she said. "You've always respected me and fought for my honor and respect among others. And I love you for it. You're my man. You're my hero. But Memphis, you can't attack a man just because he disrespects me."

She kissed his chest softly.

"You're right," Memphis said. "I don't know what happened. It's like a switch in my head just clicked and I exploded. That's never happened before. I can't believe I hit Basil. I can't believe I raised my spear like that," Memphis's tear ducts overflowed, releasing a flood down his quivering lips.

"Do you think I was going to kill him, Abby?"

"No, Memphis. I don't think so," his wife replied softly.

"Praise God for Jonah," Memphis said. "Praise God for him."

The couple held each other tightly as Memphis sobbed uncontrollably.

"I'll talk with Basil tomorrow," Memphis said shaking. "I'll try to make amends. I'll even beg for his forgiveness. In fact, I'm going to apologize to the entire group. Tonight, though, I just need to be with my Savior."

Memphis exited the tent and walked down toward the river's edge. Looking out into the jungle, he was reminded of God's calling on his life.

"Lord," Memphis prayed softly, "you sent me out here to show your love to the world, and now I've shown the exact opposite to a man you created. Forgive me, Jesus. Take away my pride and my anger and help me be the man you've called me to be. Let me show to others the love that you have always shown me. I pray that you will give me another chance to be a witness to this group and continue to guide us to the Isconahua so that they, too, might come to know you."

Memphis sat quietly in the sand by the river until his eyelids grew heavy and he slowly made his way back to his tent. Holding his wife, he fell asleep within seconds.

Night closed in on the campsite, and all were thought to be sleeping.

By three the following morning, the entire party was awake. Memphis and Abigail were washing their faces and brushing their teeth at the side of the river, while Grace filtered a few liters of water. Jonah, much more capable than he had been on his first night in the jungle, quickly packed up his tent with little help from Noah who was in a foul mood thanks to a restless night.

The morning routine to which they had recently adapted kept them from paying attention to much outside of their routine. No one had even noticed yet that someone was missing.

"Hey, where's Basil?" Jonah nonchalantly called out to no one in particular.

Noah looked around, as did the others.

"Where's Alejo?" Grace asked.

Jonah noticed that there were, in fact, two people missing.

"Alejo!" Jonah shouted. "Basil!"

"Well, they've already got their tents packed up," Abigail observed.

"They can't be far," Noah said. "I mean we are pretty much in the middle of nowhere."

"Maybe they went down the street to get some coffee from Starbucks," Jonah joked.

"I hope they bring me a cup," Noah chimed in. "A venti vanilla cappuccino would really hit the spot this morning."

"I could use a hot chocolate and a cinnamon roll," Jonah laughed.

"Good one," Noah encouraged.

The two brothers continued to exchange breakfast wishes from the States – an Egg McMuffin, doughnuts, pancakes, breakfast burrito, biscuits and gravy – all sounded too good to even dream about in the middle of the Amazon jungle. The mere thought of those American delicacies sent Jonah and Noah laughing until they could barely breathe.

"The boat is gone," Memphis solemnly called out from the beach.

The weight of his crisp yet soft words carried throughout the group, leaving them quiet and stunned like a family that just came home to find that their house had been burglarized. They walked slowly to the beach. There, they saw what they already knew to be true. The boat, along with Basil and Alejo, was missing.

"What do you think happened?" Grace asked.

"Do you think they were kidnapped by natives?" Jonah asked.

The group began to work through various hypotheses in their minds, the obvious explanation known intuitively by all. No one but Memphis, however, dared to express the awful truth.

"They left without us," he said.

"Left us?" Grace asked, not wanting to believe it.

"They abandoned us, Grace," Abigail said. "Basil and Alejo have taken the boat and stranded us out here on this beach with no way of leaving."

"Why? Why would they do that?" Jonah asked.

"I think it's pretty obvious," Noah answered. "They left because of what Memphis did to Basil yesterday. I might have left, too."

Memphis hung his head, conceding in his own mind that Noah's harsh assessment of the situation was accurate.

"I didn't do anything to him, though," Jonah said. "Noah didn't do anything. Grace didn't do anything. Abigail didn't do anything. Why did they leave all of us?"

"Basil probably offered Alejo more money," Abigail said. "And I'm sure that Alejo was eager to travel with a lighter load. They'll reach the Isconahua twice as fast without us and our packs."

Memphis looked up and began to examine the faces of the marooned group. He, more than anyone, understood their circumstances. The likelihood of another boat passing by was slim. He looked, in turn, upon the faces of Jonah, Grace, Noah, and Abigail, and registered their expressions of hopelessness. For several heavy minutes, the group silently watched each other, waiting for someone to suggest a brilliant way out of their predicament.

Beyond the trees, someone else was also watching.

CHAPTER 24

*T*HE forearm on Memphis's chest violently knocked him into the water. The man had emerged from the forest unnoticed until the moment he delivered his blow. As strong and as muscularly defined as Memphis, the nearly naked man took advantage of his momentum, knocking the blond missionary off his feet and slamming him into the shallow river behind him. Memphis struggled to catch his breath as his mind raced for understanding. He stood, wiping water out of his eyes just in time to see seven sharp spears pointing directly at him. Suddenly, he knew the fear that had gripped Basil the day before.

Memphis stood quietly. His movements purposefully limited, he quickly surveyed the condition of Abigail and the rest of the group. Several other native men surrounded Jonah, Noah, Grace, and Abigail. The fear in his wife's eyes spoke volumes to Memphis. Never before had they encountered such unexpected danger.

Who were these men? What did they want? Why had they attacked? Memphis could neither ignore nor answer any of his questions.

A spear poked his back, sharply enough to nearly break skin. Memphis interpreted the signal and began to walk. The seven men guarding Memphis, including the one who had initially tackled him, led Memphis back up the riverbank to the rest of the captives. Memphis felt like a captured animal but could not understand why they had hunted him.

"What's going on, Memphis?" Abigail whispered once Memphis had rejoined the group. "Are these men part of the Isconahua tribe?"

"I don't know. I don't think they're the Isconahua. We should still be days away from their village."

"What do you think they want?" she asked.

"I don't know. I mean, if we were close to someone's village, I could see how they might feel threatened and attack us to protect their family, but no one lives out here. I can't even figure out where these men came from."

The spear jabbed Memphis's back again, this time drawing a little blood. Also prodded by spears, Jonah and Noah walked in the same direction while the girls reluctantly followed. As they headed away from the river, the forest shadows engulfed the morning illumination of the sun. The sound of the river faded behind them as the natives forced their prisoners deeper into the jungle.

The armed native men remained silent the first hour of the hike. The entourage occasionally paused long enough for the natives to drink a handful of water from a passing stream. Memphis tried his best to stay close to Abigail despite the threatening spears. Noah closed his eyes tightly and wished himself to an old corner bookstore he once visited while on vacation in Greece, a poorly conjured image constantly interrupted by the smell of animal feces and sounds of monkeys chattering and swinging in the trees above.

Mud covered Jonah's wet boots, his stomach growled relentlessly for lack of breakfast, and blood trickled down his sunburned arms from scratches left by imposing tree branches along the narrow trail – all of which reminded him that he remained a jungle rookie. A month and a half ago, he was a semi-respectable professor living in a comfortable New York City apartment. An hour and a half ago, he was a man outside his element, learning the ropes of the Amazon, all the while slowly impressing a girl so extraordinary and attractive that it was all he could do to ignore the inescapable truth that she was out of his league. Suddenly, he had not only lost all gained ground, finding himself right back in the role of the greenhorn city boy lost in the wild, but moreover he had stumbled into a situation that could likely lead to his imminent death.

After a three-hour hike that left the five captives exhausted, terrified, and dehydrated, the trip came to an abrupt halt. Though concealed for the moment, an apparent destination had been reached. Memphis looked up, his eyes affording him an obscured view of a small village beyond the trees just in front of him.

CHAPTER 25

ARRANGED in a circle, the humble jungle homes seemed to effectively protect the inhabitants from outside threats. A large fire burned in the middle of the enclosed ring of huts. The smell of recently cooked fish lingered, while the lost sound of the river and the forgotten light of the sun simultaneously returned as they entered the clearing. Jonah squinted his eyes as he adjusted to the bright sky. In front of him, the Angosto River ran past the village.

A gentle stir of men, women, and children took place just beyond the huts. Motivated once again by spears, the hostages moved toward the commotion. Without revealing the purpose of the kidnapping or the ensuing trip through the jungle, the native men forcefully led the group to a hut previously unnoticed by Memphis. The small shelter, which was elevated from the ground, stood apart from the main circle of huts and a noble air surrounded it as well as the man who sat within.

The men and women were pushed to the ground just

outside the hut's entrance. Jonah heard rustling inside, which preceded the grand entrance of an aged warrior, obviously the village chief. Wearing a thin piece of bark beaten into an inflexible cloth around his waist, the man also sported a crown of bright feathers and several tattoos penned with thorn and ink. After solemnly examining the prisoners seated anxiously at his feet, the warrior descended from his hut and began to pace around the incarcerated company.

Abigail brushed caked dirt from her forehead. She usually didn't mind the jungle appearance, but under the circumstances, she strangely found herself desiring a warm bath somewhere on the other side of the world. Anywhere. Grace shared similar sentiments. Within their first five minutes sitting in front of the chief's hut, she had killed more than three dozen mosquitoes, each of which had left a disgusting spot of blood somewhere on her bare arms and legs.

While Memphis contemplated whether or not he should try to communicate with the leader of the tribe, the chief motioned toward the strong man who had earlier knocked Memphis into the river. The strong man gave his report, informing the aged warrior of their adventure to the Piedras River. Noah's spirit lifted, happy that he was finally hearing a native dialogue, his purpose for coming to the jungle. He watched intently as the strong man spoke.

The strong man shared with the chief how their monthly routine fishing trip to the distant river had turned into an unprecedented discovery of people colored and dressed differently from anything they had ever seen. Recognizing the outsiders as an obvious threat – for most different things do, indeed, prove threatening – the fishermen had no choice but to capture the imposing outsiders and haul them through the jungle to their chief. Surely he would know exactly how to handle the dangerous light-skinned people.

As the strong man related his story to the chief, divulging every detail of their journey, Memphis's head lifted and he looked at his wife. Abigail turned to search Memphis's eyes. The two missionaries understood every word that was being said. Were they dreaming? Memphis forced his mind to overcome his physical exhaustion and figure out the riddle. It wasn't magic. It wasn't a miracle. It was Harakmbut. This unknown people spoke the same dialect as the Amarakaeri of Duba.

CHAPTER 26

*P*RIOR to Memphis and Abigail locating the village of Duba, only six known Amarakaeri villages existed. Three of the villages, Shintuya, Masenawa, and Boca Imimbari, rested on the Madre de Dios River. The Colorado River boasted two other communities, while a sixth was located on a tributary of the Colorado. With the discovery of Duba on the Manu River, all current river maps had become outdated. Now, four years later, another family of the Amarakaeri tribe stood feet away from Memphis and Abigail, speaking the same tribal tongue of the Duba families.

Memphis patiently bided his time, hoping that Abigail would do the same. He meant to take advantage of his perceived ignorance in order to learn the genuine intentions of their captors. Up to this point, his eavesdropping only afforded him an accurate recount of his group's capture three hours earlier. Now, however, the time had arrived for the chief's response. This, Memphis surely wanted to hear.

The strong man terminated his pacing and storytelling, assuming a seat on the edge of the hut to the left of the chief. The rest of the men lowered their spears a bit, relaxing from their role of guards as they leaned in to hear the grand warrior's decision.

Silence reigned, with the pounding of Jonah's frightfully nervous heart as the loudest sound. He felt like a defendant waiting for the jury's verdict. Discerning wisdom and difficult times within the lines of the chief's face, studying the feathers extending out of his apparently earned crown, and his hard stare colored with wrinkles, each one telling a different story of unconventional battle, Jonah sadly understood that he did not have a jury of his peers. His fate rested with a man he did not understand, a man who could not understand him.

Leisurely and yet with great dignity and resolve, the chief stood in preparation to deliver his ruling. One at a time, he peered into the despairing eyes of the strangers before him. He then looked at his men, the strong man in particular, and began to address them, purposefully ignoring the lighter skinned intruders.

To Jonah and Grace, the speech sounded like nothing more than gibberish, except that each understood it was significant gibberish that would communicate whether they would live or die. Noah strangely continued to enjoy the unique opportunity of listening to a real jungle chief rattling off native words. Memphis, on the other hand, secretly interpreted every word.

The chief began by agreeing with the initial assessment

that outsiders posed a serious and dangerous threat. Unknown meant unpredictable. Families needed protection. The chief reminded the guards that their village knew enemies and had enough of them already. A new tribe, a tribe not from the jungle, suggested nothing but probable damage to their way of life and, perhaps, the loss of their own lives. Total risk. No reward. After little deliberation, the chief announced his verdict.

"E'batiaraka'," the chief concluded. *Kill them.*

Abigail's jaw dropped. As always in times of crisis, she immediately looked toward Memphis. At the same moment, the strong man forcefully lifted Memphis up from the ground, his grip on Memphis's arm. The shaking spears of the other native men prompted the rest of the seated group to stand as well. Turning the execution over to the young warriors, the chief began to walk back into his hut.

"Pai'da ea' ke'," Memphis deliberately pronounced in perfect Harakmbut. *Please don't do this.*

The chief froze. He turned around and curiously stared at Memphis. The strong man instantly let go of the missionary's arm, while the spears of the rest of the men fell to the ground. Abigail breathed a momentary sigh of relief, while the rest of the party searched their faces for clues as to what had just happened.

"Pai'da ea' ke'," Memphis repeated.

The Amarakaeri men looked at one another in absolute confusion. How could this white man with strange clothes speak their language? The makeshift courtroom seemed blanketed by silence. Then, suddenly, conversation erupted on all sides.

Interrupting one another with every word, the Amarakaeri men began to speak to Memphis as fast as they could. Question after question, the strong man and the other guards excitingly asked Memphis about his unexpected ability to speak Harakmbut, his purpose for coming to their jungle, the location of his village, and, of course, the origin of his long, blond hair. While genuinely curious, none of them gave Memphis time to answer. The Amarakaeri simply crowded around, somewhat pleasantly interrogating him and occasionally playing with the curls in his hair. Memphis felt like the latest exhibit in a New York City museum. Finally, the chief brought order to the chaotic inquiry.

"Be'a inomey?" the chief asked Memphis. *Who are you?*

Taking a deep breath and choosing his words carefully, Memphis began to introduce himself and explain the group's presence on the beach where they were found. From the details of his involvement with Duba and the Amarakaeri to the backgrounds of Jonah, Noah, and Grace, Memphis reserved no secrets in his presentation. He gave special attention to his friendship with Artone, hoping that the chief would see his desire to form similar relationships with his village. For more than twenty minutes, Memphis told the men everything.

He told them everything, except what he knew of the Isconahua and his plan to find them.

CHAPTER 27

*I*NSIDE the hut, Jonah felt safe for the first time in hours. His back free of spears, the guards walking in the other direction, and the intimidating expressions of the chief a mere memory, Jonah's situation had greatly improved. Another crowd inquisitively gathered around the hut, intrigued by the outsiders. As the rest of the members of the newly discovered Amarakaeri village became aware of their visitors, they unashamedly spied on their every movement. Jonah settled into a seated position on the floor of the exposed hut, where Grace met him.

As Abigail with Memphis, Grace sat close to Jonah, eager for the feeling of protection a familiar man could bring. Jonah instinctively placed his arm around Grace who naturally fell into his embrace. She was surprised at how comfortable she felt with a man she barely knew.

"I was so scared, Jonah," she confessed. "I've never been so afraid in my life. I can't stop shaking."

Jonah looked down and noticed Grace's shivering hands. He gently strengthened his hold on Grace's shoulder.

"I thought they were going to kill us," she continued. "I thought they were going to kill you."

"Me too," Jonah admitted.

"Were you scared, Jonah?"

"Extremely scared, Grace. I felt as though my heart was beating so loudly that the chief might kill me just to quiet it."

A faint smile appeared on Grace's face.

"I don't know how much more of this rollercoaster I can take," she said. "My emotions are a wreck. First Memphis tries to kill Basil. Then, Basil and Alejo take the boat and strand us in the middle of nowhere. A bunch of men jump out of the bushes with spears, capture us and force us to hike three hours to their tiny, hidden village. There, a chief seems to command them to kill us, and now, we're free again, but miles away from our destination and without our belongings."

"It'll be alright, Grace," Jonah said. "It'll be alright."

Jonah had no idea whether or not things would be alright and he knew that Grace knew he didn't. Still, he felt as though he needed to reassure Grace with absolute conviction. Likewise, Grace didn't concern herself with Jonah's power to guarantee his promise – she was comforted by hearing it.

On the other side of the medium-size hut loaned to the group by the chief, Noah found a place to sit on the floor. He rubbed his face with his dirty hands, trying to clear his mind and forget everything he had felt moments before. Casting off his fear and anxiety, Noah strived to refocus.

"What did you say to the chief, Memphis?" Noah asked.

"I told him who we were and that we had good intentions," Memphis replied.

"How is it that you can speak their language?"

"This is an Amarakaeri village. The same people group we served with for four years in Duba."

"They speak the same language?"

"Yes."

"Did you know that there was an Amarakaeri village this far up on the Piedras River?"

"No. No one did. Of course, no one knew about the Amarakaeri in the Duba village either."

Jonah joined the conversation.

"Are these the people you came here looking for?" he asked.

"No, they are a different tribe," Memphis replied. "The men who spotted the Isconahua reported their location on the other side of the Angosto River."

"How many different tribal groups are out here?" Grace asked.

"It's hard to say," Memphis answered. "However, in light of the recent sighting of the Isconahua and the fact the we just found another Amarakaeri village, we can assume there are still several native tribes out here yet to be contacted."

"Are the tribes enemies?" Abigail asked Memphis.

"The chief said that they had enough enemies already and didn't need any more when referring to us, so I suppose there are enemy tribes," Memphis clarified.

"I wonder who their enemies are," Noah interjected.

The strong man returned and engaged Memphis in a conversation as Abigail listened. Excluded by their ignorance of Harakmbut, the rest of the group quietly listened, trying to gain some insight into the nature of the dialogue based on Memphis's facial expressions. Five minutes later, the strong man left.

"What did he say?" Jonah asked.

"He said we can stay," Memphis answered.

"So they're not going to kill us?" Grace asked.

"No."

Grace released her breath.

"Not that I'm not thrilled about living and all, but do we really want to stay here?" Noah asked. "I mean, aren't we still trying to get to the Isconahua?"

"That's right," Grace said. "My assignment is to photograph the Isconahua. Should we ask for their help finding them?"

"I understand what you're saying," Memphis began. "However, I don't think it's wise for us to leave right away. The chief is allowing us to stay, but that doesn't mean he trusts us yet or that we're free to go. He's watching. He wants to know who we are and what we want. If we try to leave, they might just capture us all over again. And if we mention the Isconahua, well, honestly, we might inadvertently imply that we're friends with another native village that may not be friends with them."

Jonah nodded, trying to take it all in.

"So, what do we do for now?" Noah asked.

"For now, we just live with them," Memphis replied. "We will work with them, hunt with them, and talk with them. Until they know us, they likely won't allow us to leave. And until we know them, we cannot, under any circumstance, tell them about the Isconahua."

CHAPTER 28

$\mathcal{D}$EPRIVED of their backpacks, sleeping bags, tents, and mosquito nets that had been left at the beach during their capture, the newest residents of the Amarakaeri village spent their first night in the small hut, lying on the bamboo floor inches apart from one another. Sleep was difficult that night. Stiff, aching backs and uneasy spirits prevented sleep in most of the party, while Jonah's close proximity to Grace, though not exactly cozy or intimate, occupied his thoughts and emotions, effectively preventing him from closing his eyes for more than a few minutes at a time. Just a couple of feet away from Noah and Jonah, Memphis and Abigail slept fitfully through the night.

Promptly at four in the morning, the strong man arrived at the guest hut and stood just outside the entrance. Memphis immediately popped up from the floor, stepped outside and stood on the dirt beside the Amarakaeri man in order to properly welcome him. Abigail awoke and quickly stood beside her husband to greet their unexpected guest.

"Omieate," Memphis said. *Good morning.*

The strong man stared into Memphis's eyes, still hoping for further understanding of his ability to communicate in Harakmbut.

"Omieate," he finally reciprocated.

During the early exchanges between Memphis and the man who had tackled and captured him less than twenty-four hours earlier, the rest of the exhausted group began to move. Noah rubbed his neck, his facial grimace betraying the stiffness he felt.

"I don't think I slept but an hour the whole night," he said hoarsely to anyone listening.

"Me neither," Grace said.

She removed the sleep from the corner of her eyes with the index finger of her right hand. Lacking a change of clothes, Grace merely buttoned the top two buttons of her sleeveless camping shirt that she had loosened to enjoy the cool breeze in the midst of the humid night. Jonah watched Grace through squinted eyes that relentlessly fought the invading sunlight emerging from the far side of the narrow river running about one hundred yards from their hut.

Even without make-up, she still looks absolutely amazing, Jonah thought to himself. But by the time he finished admiring Grace's early morning portrait of beauty, Jonah realized that he remained the only one who had yet to stand and greet the strong native man waiting outside their hut. With groans for his back pain alternating with deep song-like yawns, Jonah stood and walked stiffly across the wooden floor to greet a man whose language he didn't speak. Unsure of whether or not a handshake was appropriate, he simply nodded at the man.

"Omieate," the man said to Jonah.

"A mocha latte," Jonah replied.

"Not bad," Memphis encouraged. "You'll be speaking Harakmbut in no time."

Jonah smiled, nodded once more at the man and Memphis, and then walked past them both to a cluster of trees where he relieved himself. Memphis apologized for his behavior to the strong man who assured Memphis that those trees often served that purpose. Grace giggled at Jonah who, upon finishing, silently walked through the group again, climbed into the hut, moved back to his sleeping spot, and tried once more to sleep. Along with everyone else standing just outside the hut, the strong man curiously watched Jonah's every move. Memphis quickly engaged the Amarakaeri man in conversation in an effort to distract him as well as to get to know him.

"Mepuru huadik?" Memphis asked. *What is your name?*

"Ba'tey," he answered.

Finally, the strong Amarakaeri warrior/fisherman/hunter had a name. Ba'tey. Memphis nodded before proceeding to introduce himself, Abigail, Noah, and Grace again. Pointing to the now-snoring Jonah, he also presented Jonah once more. Ba'tey attempted to repeat each name as he heard it. To make things easier on him, Memphis taught Ba'tey the Harakmbut name he had received from the Amarakaeri in Duba.

"Donayo Budteré," he said.

"Budteré," Ba'tey quickly repeated. "Budteré."

Ba'tey laughed heavily, showing his smile for the first time. He grabbed Memphis's hair as he said his name over and over again.

"Budteré. Budteré. Budteré."

Jonah looked up from his sleep to observe the racket. He had no idea why the native man kept repeating the word, "Budteré." He did know, however, that the man who had intended to kill them yesterday now stood outside their hut, laughing with Memphis. Jonah's yawn interrupted his smile. As long as Memphis was there speaking Harakmbut with the chief and the strong man, Jonah knew he could sleep soundly. Memphis would take care of everything. Jonah closed his eyes to return to his dream.

CHAPTER 29

"COME on now. Get up. Get up, get up, get up."

The voice carried excitement and a degree of volume that would prove unpleasant to anyone trying to sleep. The sun crept through the leaves of the roof from directly above, revealing the time of day. Along with the verbal alarm clock, other noises gradually became evident. The river continued to run just a hundred yards to the east, a flight of macaws sang overhead, a pack of children's feet scampered by, and an annoying voice continuously called out, "Get up, already."

Jonah's senses slowly awoke, his eyesight returning last, just in time to disclose the identity of the obnoxious voice. His older brother Noah was staring right at him.

"Come on, Jonah," he said. "You're missing it. You're missing everything. Get up."

"What, Noah, am I missing?" Jonah stretched his arms and

legs, showing signs of frustration rather than urgency.

"Memphis and Ba'tey went fishing. They trapped three alligators. Real, live, jungle alligators. They're bringing them up the riverbank right now, as we speak."

"Enough. I'm coming already. Just stop shouting. I'll come and see the crocodiles."

"Alligators, Jonah. Alligators. And I'm not shouting."

Noah left the hut, bouncing with anticipation to the edge of the village, which, at a slightly elevated position, looked down upon both the riverbank and the river. From there, Noah could easily see Memphis and Ba'tey rowing downriver in the humble dugout canoe. Memphis sat at the point position with Ba'tey in the back, both rowing with small wooden oars. A small boy grabbed the tip of the canoe when it ran against the sand of the bank, tying it to a tree stump with rope made of tree bark.

One after another, Memphis tossed the three alligators onto the beach. Standing up, he and Ba'tey looked like identical twins. Both stood more than six feet tall, with smooth complexions, long hair, ripped muscles, and smeared alligator blood on their chests. Only the distinct facial features of the Amarakaeri people and Memphis's blond hair betrayed their lack of kinship.

"They're not that big," Jonah said.

Jonah had approached Noah from behind him in time to see Memphis and Ba'tey standing next to one another on the bank.

"I thought the alligators would be bigger than that," he said.

"Abigail said that the whole village will have food for two days from these small alligators," Noah responded, refusing to conceal his sarcasm.

Jonah shrugged his shoulders.

"I'd rather eat a cheeseburger," he said.

Jonah took his attention off the alligators, which Memphis and Ba'tey carried up the bank to the village. Jonah surveyed the village, seeing the people and their huts in the clear day for the first time. Various circles of women gathered around four different fires scattered between the huts, apparently cooking lunch. All the men seemed to have gone elsewhere. Jonah assumed they had ventured to work, though he had little idea what kind of jobs native men held.

Were there bosses and employees and offices of some type? Were there paychecks issued in the form of chickens or monkey bones or something? A morning, barefoot commute through the muddy trails? Lunch breaks, sick days, 401-K plans? Jonah's mind conjured up numerous possibilities for the realities of jungle life. For a fleeting moment, he wished he had a journal in which he could scribble down some of his thoughts. Then, his mind quickly raced to another thought. Where was Grace?

"Good morning, Jonah."

Jonah spun around to see Memphis, bare-chested, barefoot, and smiling. Two alligators lay at his feet, quite dead. Jonah smiled back at him, though he secretly hated it when people said "good morning" during the afternoon, the implication being that he had slept too late. It made him feel lazy, especially coming from a man who had spent the morning trapping and killing alligators in the Amazon jungle.

"Hey, Memphis," Jonah replied. "Looks like you've been busy today."

"We had a good hunt. Have you ever tasted alligator meat?"

Jonah thought about the Italian restaurant in New York City and the chicken cannelloni that he frequently ordered on

Friday nights, sitting there all dressed up, talking with Noah about books and women and their father.

"No," Jonah simply answered.

"Well, you just might like it," Memphis said. "We'll cook some tonight."

Jonah nodded in agreement. Memphis sensed that Jonah lacked a desire to continue their surface conversation and excused himself. Jonah watched Memphis haul the alligators to the chief's hut where Ba'tey had already delivered the other catch. The chief merely looked at the alligators before dismissing the hunters. The gesture indicated that Memphis had earned a bit of respect for himself and his companions, and at least one more day in which the Amarakaeri men would refrain from killing them.

The taste of alligator meat aside, Jonah knew that this was a good thing. He actually found himself certain that he wanted to live another day.

Memphis walked past him again after leaving the chief's house.

"I better go wash this mess off of me before I go see Abigail," he said. Jonah nodded again.

As Memphis made his way down to the river, Jonah watched intently. There was an undeniable way about Memphis and everyone noticed it. Memphis was sure. He was a man who knew exactly who he was, allowing him to confidently carry himself in everything he did.

As Memphis stretched, muscles on his back, arms, shoulders, and chest rippled beneath his sweat and natural tan. His long, unkempt blond hair screamed that this man lived an untamed and uncommon adventure. His bare feet reminded observers that the jungle was not too tough for him, his body would pass any endurance test. And, of course, alligator blood stained across his skin bestowed upon him a sense of the wild courage enjoyed exclusively by fierce warriors and bold soldiers.

Jonah admired Memphis from afar and admired him immensely. How does a boy grow into such a man? Where does one learn that kind of self-awareness? What allows Memphis to live such a different life from that of his own? Jonah wondered if the difference between them might have anything to do with the God that Memphis preached. Suddenly, Jonah's insecurities multiplied, reminding him that he did not belong. Not only did he not belong in the undomesticated jungle, he did not belong among such honorable and inspiring company. Memphis lived above him in an extraordinary world made more extraordinary by his mere presence. Jonah wondered, not for the first time, how he measured up to Memphis in the others' eyes.

"Maybe you should join him, Jonah."

Jonah awoke from his dazed fixation on Memphis to see Grace standing next to him. She was wearing the same khaki shorts and green tank top she had on when the Amarakaeri men had captured them. She held her hair up with her hand so as to keep her neck cooler. Her smooth skin appealed to Jonah's aesthetic senses, as did the rest of her toned body. Jonah found himself staring into her enchanting eyes for a long, drawn-out moment before he finally responded.

"Join him in what?" he slowly asked.

"Maybe you should go down to the river and bathe with Memphis," Grace said. "It might help you wake up a little."

Jonah hated himself for sleeping in and sending Grace the impression that he was nothing more than a lazy city boy unable to adapt to the early jungle schedule. Even if such a description fit him perfectly, he didn't want her to know it.

"Yeah, I guess I slept in kind of late today," he said.

"You needed your rest. After all, we were almost killed yesterday."

Grace gently touched Jonah's arm when she smiled at him. Jonah appreciated her understanding. With her there, Jonah quickly became more optimistic about his first day in an indigenous village. Maybe he would just spend all day learning about Grace. They could swim in the river, rest in the shade of an orange tree, or simply watch the sun descend behind the tree line. Jonah smiled as he decided to invite Grace on a walk. Before he could, however, Ba'tey interrupted him.

"E'tiakno e'matiogka'," he instructed. *We're going to hunt.* Ba'tey thrust a bow and a set of arrows into Jonah's hands. "Budtere ea' e'tiak," he continued. *Memphis said you should come with us.*

Although Jonah could not understand a word the strong man said, he began to think that his plans with Grace would have to wait. Just before he could employ some sort of sign language in an attempt to inquire what they would do, Memphis showed up and translated.

"The chief wants Ba'tey and me to go get some more food," he said. "I think he was pretty happy about the alligators and thinks that I'm a good-luck charm or something. So, we're going hunting, and I think you should come with us."

Jonah thought the invitation sounded just like the sort of thing that a man says to another man at the prompting of his wife. "Maybe you should invite Jonah," he could imagine Abigail saying to Memphis. "He's pretty lonely and depressed, you know," she would say. However, in this case, Memphis could not have been more sincere, for the invitation was his own idea. He truly wanted Jonah to go hunting with him.

CHAPTER 30

As Jonah's arrow soared through the humid air, he watched as if it were moving in slow motion. The seemingly defenseless prey, an ugly wild turkey, sat peacefully, perched on a low branch. In a jungle typically saturated with the noises of animal calls and rushing river currents, Jonah's shot seemed to usher in a brief period of quiet. For a moment, tranquility prevailed.

Inching closer and closer to the bird, the arrow fought through the afternoon breeze, pursuing its kill. It spun as it traveled, flaunting its colorful tail feathers, the wild turkey oblivious to the approaching threat.

Jonah held his breath, surprised that the arrow was actually headed toward its mark. During the two hours they had trekked through the forest tracking animals, both Ba'tey and Memphis had succeeded in adding notches to their hunting belts, a hog and a pair of monkeys respectively. Jonah, on the other hand, merely had managed to lose four hand-carved arrows, skillfully crafted by natives but unskillfully fired into the brush by this novice. This one, though, had a chance. Jonah quietly willed the arrow to the breast of the bird.

A faint tap. The brushing of wings signaling the prey's quick escape. Losing momentum too soon, the arrow, while on target, had hit the breast of the turkey, though failing to pierce its skin as if the turkey wore some sort of bulletproof vest. Bouncing off the bird and sending the turkey to flight and escape, the arrow fell as quickly as it had ascended. Leaves rustling as the arrow dropped to the ground, falling through the branches underneath. And a sigh behind the closed eyes and grimaced face of the hunter. When it landed at the feet of the hunting party, the sound the arrow made as it hit the ground interrupted Jonah's sigh. Ba'tey's hearty laugh quickly followed.

"Great aim!" Memphis immediately exclaimed. "You hit it, Jonah. You hit it alright."

Ba'tey continued to laugh. His laugh escalated in both speed and volume, as he bent over, holding his stomach, laughing heartily.

"Don't worry about it, Jonah," Memphis continued. "You just need a little more *oomph* next time."

"E'nahuae e'mai' nogiti Masato," Ba'tey said, laughing. *You need to drink more Masato.*

Since Memphis didn't translate for Jonah, Jonah ignored Ba'tey, handing his bow to Memphis as he quietly reached down to retrieve the fallen arrow, which he also gave to Memphis. Ashamed and embarrassed, Jonah walked past the other hunters and started down the trail back toward the village. The ever-lingering question present in Jonah's mind since the day he stepped into Alejo's boat resurfaced once more: What in the world was he doing in the Amazon jungle?

Three weeks after the escape of Jonah's defenseless turkey, the once amusing anecdote had lost much of its entertainment value, finally enabling Jonah to leave his hut without encountering a group of children reenacting the entire hunting event, complete with all its mishaps. He had gotten over the embarrassment, but it was obvious to him that the villagers considered him an outsider.

Memphis went hunting or fishing with Ba'tey every day. Noah spent nearly every waking hour with Aratbuten, a man of his own age, who was helping him learn the Harakmbut language. Even Grace, through working alongside the women of the village, was picking up the language. She and Abigail blended nicely into the community and never seemed bored. It appeared to Jonah that his entire party felt quite at home in this jungle village with the exception of himself, who still spoke only English and that only rarely.

Jonah eased out of his hut, dipping his head into the afternoon sunlight. Except for an occasional lunch of fish and rice cooked by the ladies a few huts down, the jungle didn't offer much to lure Jonah outside of the group's hut prior to two o'clock each day. Noah kept encouraging Jonah that he would soon find his niche in the Amarakaeri village. What Jonah hoped to find, however, was a boat traveling downriver.

Jonah surveyed the village, one of the most boring and depressing tasks of his day. For three weeks now, he had observed the same native people doing the same primitive things all day every day in the same tribal village. Nothing changed. No one changed.

Jonah glanced over at Aratbuten's hut. Noah sat on the ground in his once new camping pants, the legs now unzipped, affording him a pair of khaki shorts. He wore no shirt, no shoes, and his ever-growing beard was covered in dirt. He scribbled wildly in a notebook while Aratbuten spoke nonstop. Well, perhaps some people do change a bit, Jonah thought. His own brother had found his element.

Just about to turn away from the language class in search for a place to urinate, Jonah stopped. He looked back at Noah. Something quite peculiar caught his eye. Although his previously refined older brother sat bare-chested, barefoot, unshaven, and messy in the dirt a mere two feet away from an unknown native man speaking a strange indigenous dialect, something else, something less obvious captured Jonah's attention and curiosity.

What, exactly, was Noah doing? Jonah slowly made his way toward Noah and Aratbuten, pausing occasionally to think through things, unembarrassed by the fact that he began to talk to himself aloud.

"What's he doing?"

"He's just learning the language like he does everyday," Jonah answered himself. "What's the big deal?"

"He usually just sits and talks with Aratbuten."

"Yeah, well, that's all they're doing now."

"No. Something is different."

Jonah quickened his approach. Squinting his eyes, he closely examined Noah.

"He's writing," Jonah quietly said aloud, finally understanding what seemed so strange. "He's writing," he said again. "He's writing!" Jonah exclaimed. "He's got a notebook and a pen, and he is writing!"

Jonah ran the last few yards to his brother.

"Where did you get that notebook?" he asked immediately.

The interruption startled Noah. Aratbuten stopped talking for the first time in half an hour. Both looked up at Jonah.

"Excuse me?" Noah politely asked.

"The notebook and pen," Jonah began, "where did you get it?"

Captured by the Amarakaeri more than three weeks earlier when Ba'tey knocked Memphis into the river, the group of outsiders had hiked through the forest to the village with nothing more than the clothes they had slept in the night before. With no mosquito nets, mats or sleeping bags, the hut floor served as their bed. Without a toothbrush or bar of soap, the group depended solely upon the river water for all their hygiene needs, using leaves on their longer toilet trips. No one had changed clothes in more than twenty days, shaving was out of the question for both sexes, the luxuries of books and flashlights were unheard of, and Jonah had all but forgotten about writing until he saw the notebook Noah was using as a rough draft for an Harakmbut dictionary.

Noah smiled, enjoying the expression of shock now planted on his little brother's face. Without a word to Jonah, Noah turned to Aratbuten and graciously excused himself with flawless execution of the language.

"Follow me," he said, taking hold of Jonah's arm.

Noah led Jonah across the village to the back of their hut. Five large camping backpacks leaned against the outer bamboo wall.

"Our backpacks!" Jonah blurted out. "They found our backpacks!"

Noah smiled broadly. He had been looking forward to this surprise since noon.

"How did this happen?" Jonah asked.

"Memphis," Noah said. "Memphis had Ba'tey lead him back to the beach to search for the packs. They left about four o'clock this morning, found them exactly how we had left them, and they carried every single one of them through the forest, making it back to the village around lunchtime."

"Memphis," Jonah repeated. "Of course."

CHAPTER 31

*T*HE recovery of the backpacks cheered the entire group, especially Jonah, who carefully arranged his corner of the hut with his mat, sleeping bag, and mosquito net. He then pulled out his books and toiletries and spent the afternoon on personal hygiene and reading. When the sun set, he closed his eyes, confident that his first night in three weeks sleeping on a surface other than a hard, wood floor would bring sweet dreams of Grace or Autumn. Instead, he spent the first hour tossing and turning on the now unfamiliar bed. Then the humidity settled in. He sat up and almost violently pulled off his T-shirt.

"It's too hot," he muttered to himself.

Jonah wiped the sweat from his forehead with the shirt. He flung the edge of the mosquito net up over his head and stood up. Three other mosquito nets crowded his. He recognized his brother's snoring coming out of the net closest to him. Next to Noah, another net draped the floor, large enough to house both Memphis and Abigail. Grace rested under the net on the opposite side of the hut. Not wanting to wake anyone, Jonah quietly maneuvered through the spider web of rope holding up the corners of the mosquito nets before carefully stepping out of the hut.

A slightly cool breeze blew by his face, producing goose bumps on the back of his neck. Jonah enjoyed a deep breath of the fresh, unpolluted air. The sound of the river rushing by the still village seemed to call out to him. Jonah turned to face the direction of the water.

Something caught Jonah's attention. A small light flickered from the edge of the forest. Jonah moved closer. What light was this? Fireflies? A flashlight? Jonah walked past the farthest hut of the village. Soon, the image became clear. A small fire consumed a carefully constructed stack of logs lying on the ground.

As he approached, he could make out the dark silhouette of a man next to the fire. As he drew closer, Jonah could make out more and more of the scene. The man was neither standing nor sitting next to the fire, he was kneeling. Jonah continued to approach quietly, drawn now by an instinctive desire to solve the mystery. The shadowy figure slowly took form as Jonah moved closer. Arms, then legs, then clothes, and hair. Finally, peeking around a tree from behind the kneeling man, Jonah recognized him. Jonah stood so close now that he could feel the heat from the fire mixing with the wind on his face. Leaning in a bit more, Jonah could not only see the man, but hear him as well.

His knees almost buried in the dirt, his arms spread wide and his face raised upward, the man was speaking passionately. It was clear that he wasn't talking to himself, but as Jonah glanced around, he saw no one else.

What is he saying? Jonah thought. He strained to listen.

"But, do we stay?" Memphis was saying. "What about the Isconahua? We need your guidance, Lord. Where do *you* want us to go?"

He stopped speaking as though he awaited an answer. Jonah finally realized that Memphis was praying. Suddenly, Jonah felt guilty for spying and decided to return privacy to Memphis. Turning to leave, however, his left foot cracked a fallen stick while his right foot rustled a pile of leaves. Jonah froze. The praying ceased.

"Jonah?"

Jonah turned to see Memphis looking straight at him.

"I saw the fire," Jonah confessed. "I was just checking it out. Once I saw that you were, well, you know, praying and all, I decided to leave. I didn't mean to interrupt you. Sorry."

Jonah turned to leave again.

"Wait, Jonah," Memphis said as he stood. "Stay for a minute."

"Are you sure?" Jonah asked. "I mean, don't you want to, you know, finish?"

"It's quite alright. Have a seat."

Memphis sat on a log facing the fire. He motioned to another log perpendicular with the one he occupied. Jonah took his cue, sitting down on the empty log. For nearly five minutes, the two men stared at the fire, refraining from speaking altogether. At last, Jonah broke the silence.

"So what are you doing out here in the middle of the night?" he asked.

"I'm just taking a retreat," Memphis said. "You know, just a night sleeping out here on the ground, trying to clear my head and talk with God for awhile."

Self-aware of his own lack of spiritual depth, Jonah merely nodded.

"I do this now and again," Memphis continued. "It's a time when I can just talk with and listen to my Savior. It helps me reflect on life…especially when life gets a little crazy."

"Yeah, it certainly is a little crazy out here," Jonah said.

Memphis looked at Jonah.

"How are you holding up, Jonah?" he asked.

"Fine."

"Really?"

"Sure, I mean, I'll be ready to go home once Noah finishes his language study, but, for the most part, I'm fine."

"You know, Jonah, we never got to talk, just you and me, I mean, about that day fishing with Basil."

Jonah looked up from the fire and made eye contact for the first time that night. Ever since meeting Memphis, Jonah had admired him. Memphis lived this strong, confident, perfect life. Everything he did, he did with utmost integrity. Everything except for attacking Basil with a spear, that is. The idea of gaining some insight into that day greatly sparked Jonah's interest.

"I've known Basil for a long time," Memphis began.

Jonah adjusted his position on the log to a more comfortable spot. He settled in for what he expected to be a long explanation.

"There's a lot of history between us," Memphis continued. "It's hard for me to look past his flaws. I know I should. I know I'm not perfect either. I just can't help, though, but to focus on his shortcomings."

Memphis took a deep breath. He moved a few logs deeper into the fire, causing the flame to elevate in height.

"Jonah, I could try to make you understand why I pushed and hit Basil, and why I took that spear to his throat as I did. But the truth is, I don't even understand it. And, that's not even the point anyway. Whatever my reason, I had no right to take our personal conflict that far. I was wrong, Jonah. I messed up. I've repented to God, and I pray that one day I'll be able to ask for Basil's forgiveness, too."

Memphis tossed a small stick into the fire. Jonah stared at him for a moment, waiting for more.

"Jonah, have you ever done something that made you feel ashamed?"

Jonah thought about his last month in the States. He would be ashamed if Memphis could somehow read his thoughts and know the truth.

"Of course," he said warily.

"Me too. I guess we all have," Memphis said. "But let me ask you, Jonah. When you feel ashamed, do you try to cover up your shame? You know, hide it?"

"Drown it," Jonah said. "I try to drown it."

Jonah sensed he could be honest with Memphis and he desired to have his respect, so he continued. "When I feel ashamed, when I think about the way I've messed up my marriage and my career, I dive into the closest bottle I can find."

Memphis nodded as though he could relate.

"I think we all devise ways of covering our shame," Memphis said. "You know what, though; we men have been doing that since the beginning of time."

"We have?"

"Yes. You know who the first man was?"

"You mean, Adam?"

"Exactly. Adam, the first man, did the one thing God commanded him not to do. And as soon as he did it, he was ashamed. And then, just like you and me, he tried to cover it up." Memphis reached out to tear a thin limb covered in leaves from a nearby tree.

"Adam tried to cover his shame with leaves," said Memphis, holding the branch up for Jonah to see.

"Leaves?"

Jonah attempted to follow the story. "I don't know…I think alcohol would've worked better."

Memphis laughed.

"Maybe, but I think we both know that neither works. In fact, Adam knew this, too. So, he hid behind a tree."

"Hid from whom? Eve?"

"No. Adam hid from God. You see, when we try to cover up our mistakes – our sin – I believe that, deep down, we're trying to hide from God. Adam couldn't though, and neither can we."

"So what happened?"

"God found Adam and showed him that only He could cover Adam's sin. You see, God doesn't just cover up our mistakes, He is able to completely free us from all of our sin. Only God can wipe the slate clean and give us a fresh beginning."

Not since going to church with his grandfather throughout elementary school had Jonah thought so much about God. He listened to Memphis though, because he knew that Memphis lived what he was saying. Jonah didn't know anyone who could talk about freedom like Memphis, simply because Jonah didn't know anyone who lived with as much freedom as Memphis did. Memphis's life was free from addiction, depression, envy, and fear. It was clear that God was the source of that freedom.

"So, Memphis, how does God free us from sin?" Jonah asked.

"With a sacrifice. His Son, Jesus Christ, who was sinless, took our sin upon Himself so that we don't have to be burdened with it anymore. Put your faith in Him, and He will forgive you of your sin. That's what I've done. I chose freedom and, by the grace of Jesus, I have been forgiven and restored. Jesus is the only one who can give you a new life. I know that's what you're searching for, Jonah. Ask Jesus for forgiveness for those things that you're ashamed of and, I promise, you'll find a new life worth living."

Jonah loved hearing Memphis talk. His words filled him with hope. However, as soon as hope beckoned, a heartbreaking thought overcame it.

"What if it's too late for me?" Jonah asked. "I mean, what if I've already missed my chance? What if I've been hiding behind the tree so long that God's not even looking for me anymore?"

Memphis moved closer, putting his arm around Jonah.

"God never leaves us, Jonah. He's right here. Tonight. Waiting for you to begin a new life with him. Jonah, it's time to start living."

CHAPTER 32

As Jonah started back toward the village, he had every intention of returning to his sleeping bag in the communal hut. His midnight walk, however, had left him even more restless than before, his mind was agitated by dozens of thoughts crashing into each other – thoughts of Grace, Autumn, and Paige; thoughts of the unwritten novel; of the college and Dr. White; of the whiskey, pain pills, and suicide – and, through it all, he kept returning to Memphis's admonition to "start living."

As he approached the village, he heard the sounds of the river again. Certain that he would not be able to go to sleep for quite some time, Jonah decided to descend to the riverbank for his own late-night retreat.

Although he had never entered the river after dark before – bathing in daylight had seemed risky enough – Jonah decided to step into the water. He was surprised by the cool nighttime temperature of the river. The mild current lightly tossed small pebbles against his ankles. He took another step, then another, wading into the river until the water covered his knees and then his shorts.

How do I receive forgiveness and freedom? Jonah kept asking himself. How do I start living?

The water reached Jonah's stomach. He stood oblivious to his previous fears of the jungle and the river life swimming all around him. With his head tilted back, his eyes fixed on the vast, colorless, and yet ever-so-bright sky, Jonah finally saw the beauty of the jungle into which he had been hastily thrust. The canopy of stars was draped over the jungle like an umbrella covering the earth, so different than Jonah had known in downtown New York where the city's lights made the stars invisible.

Jonah closed his eyes.

"God, I want the freedom that Memphis has. I'm tired of hiding from you and from life. I'm tired of trying to cover up everything that I'm ashamed of. I know that I can't hide from you anyway. You know that I'm a drunk. You know that I was a lousy husband and a lazy teacher. I'm washed-up and wasted and I have nothing left, and…I'm sorry. I believe what Memphis told me about Jesus is true. Please forgive me for wasting my life and letting other people down. I need to start over and Memphis said you could give me new life. I want to begin living today, really living. I want my life to count for something." Jonah was silent for a moment before adding, "Thank you, God, for listening."

As he opened his eyes, Jonah embraced a child-like innocence while a forgotten sense of peace danced around him like the waves of the river. Joy bubbled up inside and Jonah laughed aloud, diving into the water and bursting back through the surface as a baby entering the world.

Everything looked new, felt new. He longed for a mirror so that he could check his appearance. Did he look different? It didn't matter. One thing that Jonah knew for certain was that he was, in fact, different. With nowhere to be, Jonah stood quietly, knowing contentment, enjoying the glorious night.

"What's a man like you doing in a river like this?"

Jonah shifted his gaze from the stars to Grace's eyes. No matter how many times he looked at her, Grace's eyes always seemed to have a fresh surprise to give, a new secret to disclose.

"Well?" she asked. "What has you up so late?"

"Just enjoying life," Jonah answered. His smile showed that he welcomed the company. "What about you, Grace? You out here fishing or something?"

Grace's laugh reminded Jonah of younger, more carefree years.

"It is impossible to sleep for the heat," she said. "Abigail recommended that I take a quick dip in the river to lower my body temperature."

"I bet you were happy to get your backpack today," Jonah said, excited to be making conversation with Grace again.

"Extremely happy. I was finally able to shave my legs, wash

my hair, and bathe with soap. I feel clean for the first time in weeks."

"Good."

"Plus, you know what else was in my backpack?"

"What?"

"My camera."

Jonah smiled. He had nearly forgotten that Grace was a photographer on an assignment.

"That's great, Grace," he said. "I bet you'll take some incredible pictures of this place."

Jonah looked back up at the sky, appreciating all over again the starry night.

"It's beautiful out here," he said when he returned eye contact to Grace.

"I thought you'd never notice," she commented as she waded into the water.

Jonah read her eyes. He found no traces of sarcasm or insult. She always appeared genuinely concerned and interested. She always looked so innocent and beautiful and unequivocally seductive.

"I have been distracted lately, haven't I?" Jonah suggested.

"A little bit."

The two spoke slowly and clearly as if every word carried great significance. Jonah moved closer to her as he spoke.

"I don't belong out here, you know," he said. "This jungle… it's not me."

"Where do you belong?" Grace asked.

"I'm not sure, but I'm starting to think I'm getting closer."

As the conversation turned to lighter things, the two adults transformed into children. Jonah challenged Grace to a rock-skipping contest, while she in turn challenged him to a swimming race. Their laughter blended with the calls of the monkeys and the chirping of tree frogs. For several hours, they celebrated the night. Forgetting worries, fears, insecurities, and job assignments, Jonah and Grace flirted and played and laughed, refusing to allow the late hour to define the boundaries of their lives.

CHAPTER 33

"*H*E's not in his mosquito net."

Noah exited the hut as he called out to the rest of the group sitting by a small fire about fifteen yards away from the entrance of their humble habitat.

"He's never up this early," Abigail said. "It's not even five thirty yet."

Memphis looked around the village in search for Jonah. Noah peeked down the riverbank and into the river. Neither spotted him. Grace sat quietly, enjoying her first mug of morning coffee in nearly a month. Memphis used some of the instant coffee packs from his backpack to make a pot for the group.

"He'll turn up," Grace said. "He's probably out thinking or writing or something."

"Writing?" Noah questioned. "No, not Jonah. He hasn't written in quite some time."

"I hope he's not hurt," Memphis said. "I'm going to go check with Ba'tey. Maybe he's seen him."

"I'll go with you," Noah said.

With the men walking away, Abigail turned to address Grace.

"You seem awfully content this morning," she said suggestively.

Grace smiled and then took another sip of her coffee.

"You know, Grace, I did hear some laughing coming from the river last night. You wouldn't know anything about that, would you?"

Grace laughed out loud. Abigail too began to giggle.

"Grace? What's going on?"

"Nothing," Grace finally answered. "Well, not *nothing*. Jonah and I just talked a little last night."

"Good," Abigail said. "That's good. He hasn't spoken much of anything to anybody lately."

The girls sat quietly for a minute. Abigail waved the lid of a pan at the coals of the fire, rekindling the flames. Grace drank her coffee while replaying in her mind scenes from her night in the river with Jonah. Before Abigail could restart the conversation and pry for more details, Memphis and Noah returned.

"Ba'tey hasn't seen Jonah at all this morning," Memphis informed the women.

"He's been gone for at least an hour," Noah added.

Just as Grace began to worry for the first time that morning, Abigail spotted Jonah walking back into the village. He emerged out of the forest just behind the chief's house. With his shirt wrapped around his head to soak up the sweat dripping from his hairline, Jonah carried two large stalks of bananas over his shoulders. Taken aback, Grace, Noah, Memphis, and Abigail watched Jonah approach the village, pass the chief's hut and make his way over to their fire.

"Well, it's not pancakes and waffles or anything, but if

anybody wants some fresh bananas, breakfast is served," Jonah said, dropping the stalks on the ground in the middle of the group.

Jonah reached down and pulled a large, ripe, yellow banana off one of the stalks. Peeling it, he handed the fruit to Grace. Abigail smiled.

"Thank you, Jonah," Grace said. "Are you not going to have one?"

"No thank you. I found some sugarcane along the trail about a half hour ago on my way back to the village. I devoured about three of those things."

Memphis smiled and patted Jonah on the back.

"Thanks for breakfast, Jonah," Memphis said. He grabbed a banana and began to cut it with his knife, preparing it for frying over the fire. He then cut one for Abigail as well.

Noah couldn't stop staring at Jonah.

"Who are you?" he finally asked.

"Excuse me?" Jonah replied.

"You're up early. You're hiking around the jungle by yourself, cutting and hauling banana stalks and eating sugar cane. Who are you?"

Jonah laughed. Glancing over at Grace and then looking back at his brother, he said, "You know, Noah, it sure is beautiful out here."

"Hey, Jonah," Memphis said from the other side of the fire. Jonah turned.

"Ba'tey and some of the other guys and I are going fishing this morning," Memphis said. "You should come."

"Why not?" he answered casually.

"What about you, Noah?" Memphis asked.

"No thanks, Memphis. I think I'll keep plugging away with Aratbuten. He's a great teacher."

With Memphis translating, Ba'tey explained to Jonah the importance of silence. This was a stealth mission. Each group would inaudibly row along the shores of the secluded lake, staying extremely close to the edge of the bank. It would take the group of eight fishermen in four canoes more than an hour to row upriver to the entrance of the canal, which led to the hidden lagoon. Then, the pairs of men would split up with their weapons of choice to hunt the fish.

Since Jonah had never fished with spears or bows and arrows, Ba'tey picked him to serve as his rower. While Ba'tey stood in the tip of the small wooden canoe, his bow and arrow firmly gripped in a ready position, Jonah sat still in the back of the dugout, slowly rowing the boat around the outskirts of the lake. Occasionally, Ba'tey found it necessary to motion Jonah and instruct him to either speed up or slow down or row more quietly or hug the bank tighter. However, for the most part, Jonah fulfilled his duties without direction.

From time to time, Ba'tey fired an arrow into the lake, disturbing the still waters. Each time, the sharp arrow effectively pierced a medium-size fish that Ba'tey then brought into the boat. Nine fish later, Jonah understood the process and could even tell when Ba'tey spotted a fish worthy of his efforts. Just when he thought he had it all figured out, though, Ba'tey did something completely unexpected.

Jonah rhythmically rowed around the edge of the lagoon, waiting for Ba'tey to find his next kill. Ba'tey looked back at Jonah and motioned for him to stop rowing. Jonah complied. Without making a sound or taking his eyes off the water, Ba'tey carefully placed his bow and arrow into the boat, freeing his hands. Jonah watched intently. For a moment, Ba'tey just stood there, looking into the water like he had lost something. Then, in an instant, he suddenly dove out of the boat and into the water. Jonah unintentionally blurted out some indistinguishable phrase and then held his breath. The sound startled the other fishermen located around the lagoon and they quickly turned their attention to Jonah who sat alone in his canoe, staring into the dirty lake. Memphis was about to call out to see what had happened when Ba'tey burst out of the water.

Splashing Jonah and rocking the boat, the strong man resurfaced, raising his arms straight in the air to display his trophy. Jonah wiped the water from his eyes and looked over at Ba'tey. With both hands, he clinched the sides of a large turtle.

How had he seen the thing through this dirty water? Jonah wondered. How did he grab it? Why did he grab it? What's he going to do with a turtle?

Ba'tey climbed back into the canoe and killed the turtle by shoving the sharp tip of an arrow into the neck opening of the shell. Blood spilled from the sides of the shell causing Jonah's face to turn a shade lighter. Watching from across the river, Memphis began to laugh.

"Sahuero huatierik oro'omeytaj oy sikyo," he yelled. *We're eating turtle eggs tonight, gentlemen.*

"Sahuero huatierik," the other fishermen shouted with great enthusiasm.

CHAPTER 34

A WEEK after the Amarakaeri's feast of turtle eggs, Memphis heated up the last of his instant coffee for his traveling companions.

"We'll have to start in on Abigail's batch tomorrow morning," Memphis informed the group, all sitting and waiting patiently around the fire with their empty coffee mugs.

As had become his custom, Jonah sat next to Noah and Memphis while the girls enjoyed their morning together. For Jonah, their morning coffee usually proved to be the only time when he could sit and talk with his brother. During the day, the indigenous were usually around and English just didn't seem appropriate.

"Did you see Grace last night?" Noah asked Jonah while Memphis checked on the coffee.

Jonah looked over at Grace. Engulfed in her own conversation with Abigail, she seemed oblivious to the Frost brothers.

"Yes I did," Jonah proudly answered. "We stayed up a few hours after you all went to sleep."

"Did you go to the river again?" Noah asked.

"We did. We just swam and skipped rocks and, well, let's just leave it at that."

The two brothers laughed together.

"That's great Jonah. She seems like an amazing woman."

"She is, Noah. She's incredible. Everything about her just captivates me. I'd spend every day with her if I could."

"Well, you're on your way," Noah said. "I think you've spent just about every night with her this week."

"Not, 'just about'," Jonah corrected. "It has been every night," he bragged.

"What are you boys talking about?" Abigail interrupted.

Jonah blushed a little bit.

"Not much," he said. "What about you girls?"

"We were talking about you and Grace and your nights together in the river," Abigail boldly confessed.

Memphis and Noah exploded in laughter while Jonah and Grace blushed and smiled and tried their hardest not to look at one another.

"I think it's great," Memphis said, obviously trying to strip the moment of its awkwardness. "However, you're going to have to wait until tonight to see her again, Jonah."

"And why is that, Memphis?" Abigail asked. "What are you two off doing today?"

"Today, my love, Jonah and I are going hunting."

"We are?" Jonah asked.

"Just the two of you?" Abigail asked.

"That's right. Just me and Jonah."

Memphis poured each member of the circle a cup of coffee. Grace took a drink and then looked up at Memphis.

"What are you hunting today?" she asked.

Memphis looked at Jonah and smiled.

"Today, Jonah and I will be hunting jaguar," he said.

Since arriving in Peru, Jonah had endured dehydration, kidney stones, mosquito bites, sunburns, culture shock, language barriers, disgusting food, Spartan living conditions, humiliation, embarrassment, and the threat of loss of life. None of these discomforts, however, seemed significant in light of what Memphis was now calling him to do. Hunt jaguars? Jonah numbly followed Memphis through the jungle foliage in disbelief.

With an old, rusted machete that he had dug out of his pack that morning, Memphis led the way, clearing a path where a path had never before existed. Jonah carried two bows and four arrows, which required all of his attention, lest the long weapons get caught in the overhanging brush of the rain forest. The longer the two men worked to make progress, the higher the sun rose. Soon, the jungle heat settled in. Jonah followed Memphis's lead in removing his shirt, which meant one more thing to carry.

Memphis talked as he walked, punctuating his sentences with machete chops. He explained to Jonah that a few men had spotted a family of jaguars out this way two days earlier. Since they had already killed three wild hogs and could carry no more, they had declined the hunting invitation the exposed jaguars issued, quietly avoiding the animals, lest the jaguars decide to hunt the men. Memphis had volunteered Jonah and himself to return to the area to pick up the village's next meal. For the Amarakaeri, the jungle was their source of food and staples and hunting was as much a part of daily life as trips to the grocery store for Americans. Jonah understood this on an intellectual level, but he couldn't help thinking he'd much prefer the jaguar meat to be processed and packaged so that he and Memphis could simply pick it up using a coupon they had clipped from the morning newspaper.

Memphis and Jonah pressed on for more than three hours, fighting the brush, the bugs, and the heat. The conversation waned, as did their energy. Memphis kept his head down, focusing on tracks in the dirt. Jonah spent the time picturing

Grace, scripting in his head their future evening rendezvous.

"The tracks have ended," Memphis finally said, breaking the silence.

Both men stopped walking. The statement surprised Jonah who was unaware that his leader had been following the tracks of their prey. Suddenly he felt quite vulnerable and afraid, realizing he was standing at the end of the jaguars' trail. Memphis surveyed the area and then checked the ground again to make sure he hadn't missed anything. All jaguar traces had indeed disappeared. Undiscouraged, Memphis knew this was all part of the hunt.

"Let's set up camp here," he said.

Memphis sat on a clear spot next to a tree and leaned his sweaty back against the trunk. Jonah followed his lead, plopping down against a nearby tree so he could sit facing Memphis, leaning his back and their bows and arrows against the same tree.

"What do we do now?" Jonah asked.

"We wait. If we're lucky, we'll see or hear something that will give us a clue as to which way to keep trekking."

"And if we're not lucky?"

"Well, worst-case scenario, we'll just sit here for a couple of hours, enjoy the outdoors, and then make the long trip back empty-handed. We'll eat fish for dinner rather than jaguar, and we'll try again in a couple of days."

"Doesn't sound too bad," Jonah said.

"That's the beauty of it, Jonah. Even if you kill nothing, you can still have a successful hunting trip."

"Well, if we do see something, I think you should take the shot, Memphis. I don't want to blow it again like I did with the turkey."

"Forget about the turkey. You know how many shots I've missed while hunting out here? You just have to focus on the next one. You know, hope to shoot better the next time."

"I guess," Jonah conceded.

"I'll tell you what, if we see a jaguar, we'll both take the shot."

"That sounds good."

With their plan set, Memphis and Jonah stopped talking and began the wait. Memphis maintained a keen sense of awareness of their surroundings. He knew that each sound and movement communicated something. Eventually, one of those noises would indicate the location of the jaguar family the Amarakaeri men had spotted just days earlier. Jonah trusted that Memphis would let him know when he needed to do something. Putting his confidence in Memphis, Jonah began to drift into a light sleep.

When Jonah awoke forty-five minutes later, Memphis's arm was reaching across his face. Confused, Jonah watched as Memphis steadily took hold of one bow and one arrow from the other side of Jonah. He then positioned himself behind his tree, kneeling on his left knee. He lifted the bow and pulled the arrow taut. Now, Jonah was fully awake.

Jonah glanced around his tree to see what Memphis saw. At first, the sleep in his eyes combined with the natural camouflage of the jungle blinded him to the animal that stood a mere ten yards away. After rubbing his sleepy eyes to get a better look, he found himself staring at the first jaguar he had ever seen in his life.

The beast stood still, unmoved by the presence of hunters. Jonah turned back around, taking his eyes off of the jaguar. He looked over at Memphis who leaned closer to the animal, ready for his shot. Jonah instinctively grabbed the remaining bow and another arrow. Kneeling like Memphis, he peered around the opposite side of the tree, so as not to crowd Memphis. Both men pointed their arrows at the intimidating creature. Jonah's eyes grew big. Through his peripheral vision, he could see Memphis readjusting his arrow and then pulling it taut again. Jonah imitated the action, deciding that he would not fire until Memphis shot his arrow.

Without warning, the still beast came to life. His muscles rippled through his body when he sprang into movement like a prisoner casting off his shackles. Dirt flew into the air as the power of his leap unearthed the ground. Despite the sudden swift escape of the jaguar, Memphis watched the event unfold in slow motion. He had waited too long. He had missed his chance. Memphis sighed in disappointment and lowered his bow.

Not knowing that it is virtually impossible to hit a moving, sprinting jaguar, Jonah let go of his bowstring, setting his arrow free. Like a horizontal bolt of lightning, the arrow split the humid air, entering the thick flesh of the jaguar, inches above its hind legs. The arrow traveled into the body, the point exiting through the chest of the creature. Wounded and bleeding, the jaguar collapsed.

While the animal struggled to keep moving, Jonah intuitively reached for the remaining arrow and reloaded his bow. Before the jaguar could regain enough strength to get off the ground, Jonah stood up, moved a little closer, and fired his second shot, piercing the neck and killing the beast. The decisive blow brought a shout of excitement from Memphis who leaped out from behind his tree to congratulate the stunned victor.

Jonah cautiously approached the fallen jaguar. His chest

heaved while he tried to catch his breath. Bending down to absorb every last detail, he was awestruck by the dynamics of the battle scene. Sweat covered the jaguar's hide just as it coated Jonah's skin, while dirt caked both the jaguar's paws and Jonah's bare feet. Blood dripped around the wood of the sunken arrow, which Jonah began to slowly remove. Marveling at the sight, he dropped the arrow and peered deep into the soul of his prey. The jaguar's lifeless eyes maintained their threatening stare.

An intense sensation of deep satisfaction began to overwhelm Jonah. An unfamiliar feeling of boldness and intrepidity emerged from deep within. Jonah gloried over his prize and all that it brought him. Looking into the eye of his first kill, Jonah, for the very first time in his adult life, felt fully alive.

CHAPTER 35

"Now turn to the side so I can get the river behind you. Perfect. Now, move closer together."

Memphis, Jonah, and Noah took Grace's direction like professional models. Since Memphis had found the group's backpacks, Grace had spent every day taking pictures of each aspect of their adventure with the Amarakaeri. By now, the three men were accustomed to the routine.

"Pull your necklace out over your T-shirt, Jonah," Grace instructed.

"It's been a month since I killed that jaguar and she still won't let it go," Jonah mumbled to Noah as he pulled out his necklace. The homemade necklace Grace had strung together displayed a jaguar's tooth with two small claws on either side.

"You guys look great," Grace affirmed. "I think this memory card is almost full, so make sure you smile. Just give me a second while I switch lenses."

"Smiling shouldn't be a problem for you, Jonah," Memphis whispered among the men. "You've been beaming all morning."

Noah laughed.

"Yeah, what's going on, Jonah?" Noah asked.

"Nothing."

"Oh. Nothing. Well, that makes sense," Memphis said.

"Well, if you must know...."

"We must," Memphis said.

"Yeah, we must," Noah affirmed.

Jonah glanced over at Grace. His permanent smile doubled in size.

"I told her I loved her last night," he confessed to Memphis and Noah, never taking his eyes off the photographer.

"That's great," Memphis encouraged.

"What did she say?" Noah inquired.

"She said, 'Right back at ya,'" Jonah replied.

All three men burst into laughter. Noah put his arm around Jonah's shoulders and squeezed him tightly.

"Congratulations, little brother," he said.

"Guys, I'm ready," Grace interrupted.

The men stood close together and smiled. With the river in the background, the lens focused and the jaguar-tooth necklace showing, Grace took the picture. She removed the memory card and tucked it away in her shorts' cargo pocket.

"I'm going to reload with an empty card," she said. "Then,

I want to take one of you guys with Ba'tey. I hope it's a good one. I'm down to my last battery."

Ba'tey had arrived at the bank moments earlier. The novelty of a digital camera continued to fascinate the natives. Even after six weeks of pictures, though, Ba'tey remained the only native who dared to allow Grace to take his picture. The rest of the tribe feared that the camera somehow stole their souls. This belief became extremely popular when they noticed the instant picture of Ba'tey that appeared on the little screen on the back of the camera once Grace snapped a shot.

Memphis motioned for Ba'tey to join the group while Grace replaced the memory card. Before he could move one step, however, an unforeseen arrow flew through the air and stuck into Ba'tey's throat. Blood spurted out of the nickel-sized hole, spraying Memphis's face. The thud of Ba'tey's dead body swiftly hitting the ground rang out across the village. Before Memphis could react, another arrow cut through the clear sky and killed a second Amarakaeri man standing close to the bank. Suddenly, a host of flying arrows filled the village and chaos ensued.

"To the hut!" Memphis yelled.

Jonah sprinted to Grace and hurriedly pulled her across the village toward the hut. Noah followed his brother as fast as he could while Memphis took off the other way in search of Abigail. The group dodged men and arrows as they ran, while an army of fifteen unclothed natives from a different tribe raided the village.

The Amarakaeri warriors wasted no time in arming themselves for the battle. By the time the visiting army had murdered four men, the home team was returning fire. Another flock of arrows took flight, men from both sides falling to the ground.

Jonah kept Grace's head down while they hastily made their way to the hut. Once inside, they, along with Noah, stayed low and hoped with all their heart that Memphis would find Abigail in time. They could see Memphis checking hut after hut on the other side of the village. Finally, he found his wife.

"What's going on, Memphis?" Abigail asked, her voice quivering.

"We're under attack," he said. His strong tone somehow comforted Abigail.

"Who's attacking us?" she asked.

"I don't know. I suppose it's their enemies that the chief mentioned."

Memphis hid Abigail in the corner of the hut and used his body as a shield to cover her. Outside the relatively safe haven of the huts, men continued to fall. Although valiant warriors, the Amarakaeri proved no match for the surprise attack. Within ten minutes, the outside army had killed every Amarakaeri male over the age of twelve. Finding Memphis and Abigail as well as Jonah, Grace, and Noah, the enemies, curious about their presence, secured the foreigners as prisoners rather than killing them.

When Aratbuten, Noah's language teacher and the village's last standing man, breathed his last, the shooting ceased and the sky cleared. The naked army, now down to eleven men, immediately forced the surviving women and children, along with the light-skinned outsiders, into the open where they sat them down on the ground.

Following much discussion, the men grabbed Memphis, Abigail, Jonah, Grace, and Noah, nudged them with the dull ends of their spears and separated them from the Amarakaeri.

Grace squeezed Jonah's arm tightly, inwardly vowing to never let go. Memphis took hold of Abigail's hand while maintaining eye contact with the closest warrior. Noah glanced over his shoulder at the forest and briefly considered making a run for it.

The apparent leader of the soldiers stepped toward Memphis and grabbed him by his throat. With stern, swift motions, he jerked Memphis's head from side to side, studying his face. The leader spoke two foreign words to the rest of the men and then descended to the riverbank. The warriors obeyed their orders and pushed the five outsiders in the same direction. Less than two months after the Amarakaeri had surprised them on the beach, Memphis and the rest of the group found themselves captives once more. With spears against their backs, they crossed the river at its most narrow point, entered the forest on the other side, and fearfully began another forced march through the jungle.

Grace occasionally attempted to speak to Jonah, to seek assurance that it would all turn out alright or just to tell him that she loved him, but the guards would allow no conversation. During the five hours of stumbling through the root clusters, mud, and thorns of the non-existent trail, Grace and the rest of the group learned to walk in silence. By the time the forest showed signs of clearing, the scorching sun began to set. Purple and orange streaks beautifully smeared the sky, while the outline of the full moon revealed its form and position. The tree line faded, becoming their background rather than environment. Jonah lifted his weary head and wiped the stinging sweat out of his eyes. There before them was another native jungle village.

The army shoved the group through a large open field

into the middle of a circle of huts. Men, women, and children stopped their working, cooking, and playing to gather around the newcomers. As the warriors told their stories, family members celebrated their victory over the Amarakaeri and mourned the deaths of the men lost in battle. Finally, the leader gave a curt command and his warriors ushered the captives to a dilapidated hut located outside the village proper.

When they arrived, Memphis, Abigail, Jonah, Grace, and Noah froze. Peering inside the hut, they could not believe what they saw. Two beaten, malnourished men sat on the floor, filthy, weak, and scarcely alive. Despite the unkempt and emaciated appearance of the two men, the group recognized them at once.

"Basil? Alejo?" Memphis uttered in disbelief.

CHAPTER 36

$\mathcal{S}$TILL prevented from speaking by the warriors, the prisoners were left to their imaginations as they tried to fill in the blanks. How did Basil and Alejo end up in this village? Where was this village? Who were these people? Why did they attack the Amarakaeri? Why did they hold the outsiders as prisoners? And the most vital question on everyone's mind: Did these people plan on killing them?

After three hours, the guards took up posts outside the hut and the captives found themselves unsupervised. Finally, they could ask their questions and get some answers.

"What's going on, Basil?" Memphis began.

"Quiet," Basil said sharply. "We might not be able to see

them, but those guards are always nearby. As far as I can tell, at least two men stay awake each night to watch us. We can talk, but we should whisper."

"Sorry," Memphis said, lowering the volume of his voice considerably. "So, what's going on?"

"What does it look like? We are being held prisoner."

"Who are these people?" Memphis continued.

"The Isconahua."

"Are you sure?"

"Yes, Memphis, I'm quite sure," Basil said, refusing to conceal his condescending attitude.

Memphis realized Basil was not in the mood to be interrogated.

"Are you and Alejo alright?" Abigail asked.

Basil paused. Looking into the eyes of the women served to ease the tension and calm his temper.

"It could be much worse, I suppose," he answered, his agitation diminishing.

"What happened when you first arrived?" Memphis sincerely inquired. As much as he wanted to, he refrained from bringing up the fact that Basil and Alejo had taken the boat and stranded them on the beach two months earlier.

"They initially accepted us," Basil said. "They demonstrated signs of curiosity. They were by no means friendly, but they welcomed us, more or less, and allowed us to interact with them. We worked with them most days the first couple of weeks. In fact, I had just begun to learn some of their dialect when they put us in here."

"What caused them to suddenly change their minds?" Jonah asked.

"Well, it is a long story, but the climax is that one of the men spotted Alejo bathing in the river with his daughter. The woman is about twenty years old, and I do not think that she is married, but that does not matter. In that instant, in their minds, we became thieves and they treated us accordingly."

"Thieves of what?" Grace asked.

"Their women," Basil said. "We have been confined to this hut ever since."

Noah took a closer look at Basil and Alejo. He cringed at the sight of their lice-infested beards, blood-shot eyes, filthy skin, infected cuts, and bony bodies.

"So you two just sit in here all day long with no food or bathroom or anything?" Noah asked.

"There is a little boy that brings us water and fruit every other day," Basil said. "And the guards do not seem to mind if we step out to use the bathroom. If we were to go any further, though, I am certain they would act."

Grace pictured their friend Ba'tey falling to the ground with an arrow in his neck, an image she had not been able to dismiss since it had happened early that morning.

"I'm sure they would act," she whispered, her tone sorrowful, her face downcast. "These people are brutal."

For the next hour, Memphis and Basil exchanged experiences from the past two months, including the other Amarakaeri village, language nuances of the Isconahua, and the battle between the two tribes. Around three in the morning, the reunited group of seven travelers fitfully slept under the guard of native men and deadly spears.

_____

Basil observed one positive aspect of his two-month captivity. His fixed location in the decaying hut afforded him the very perspective he had hoped for. Every day he sat outside of the tribe so as not to influence or change their culture, unable to do anything but observe. He witnessed all characteristics of their unique culture. The way the community ate and fished and hunted and bathed and carried out their daily duties lay ever before him. He could overhear their language and smell their food. From an anthropologist's point-of-view, Basil's time living in the Isconahua village proved quite successful.

Day by day, nothing the tribe did surprised him. He felt as though he had already seen it all. That is why the next morning's activity immediately struck Basil as odd.

An hour before the village usually awoke, the men began stirring, their weapons in hand. Basil watched carefully, trying to figure out what was taking place. The army assembled and met in a large group in the middle of the circle of huts. After receiving orders from the leader, the men dispersed, dividing into four groups. Two groups ran into the forest and the other two headed toward the river. By this time, all of the prisoners were awake and joined Basil in watching the unfolding mission. Jonah was the first to notice that someone in their group was missing.

"Is Alejo using the bathroom?" he asked.

Everyone turned their attention away from the army and looked around the hut. Sure enough, Alejo was gone. Basil was just about to offer a theory as to Alejo's whereabouts when one of the groups of warriors returned from the direction of the river. Two of the men held either arm of Alejo, the other two guarding him from the rear.

"Did he try to escape?" Memphis asked.

Basil said nothing. He merely watched as the leader called back the other groups of his men. Once they returned, he led them all to the rotten hut that served as their prison for unwelcome intruders. Two men thrust Alejo to the front of the crowd. Nearly two-dozen spears pointed at his skinny torso. The leader viciously stared at the other prisoners. The short pause seemed to last an hour. Then, without warning and without a word, the leader lifted his spear, spun around to face Alejo, and drove the sharp stick into his chest.

Grace's scream covered up Alejo's final gasp for air. He died a mere foot from the front of the hut. Abigail hid her face in Memphis's chest, her tears running down his stomach. The ruthless leader showed neither remorse nor emotion. Looking back at the captives, he borrowed another spear from the man to his left. Noah instinctively backed away from the edge of the hut.

Using the tip of the spear, the leader began to draw something in the dirt, a circle with a dot in the middle. He then pointed at Basil. To the side of his first scribble, he drew another identical symbol and pointed to Abigail. One at a time, the leader drew six pictures, pointing at one of the captives after each drawing. First Basil, then Abigail, Noah, Memphis, Grace, and Jonah. Noah peered over the edge of the hut to see the sketches, recognizing the primitive symbol.

Six drawings. Six suns. Six warnings.

One last look, and then the Isconahua leader departed. His army followed, leaving Alejo's dead body on the ground outside the hut.

CHAPTER 37

THEORIES and speculations abounded throughout the rest of the day. The presence of Alejo's body and the six suns left everyone, including Memphis, fearing one thing: death. And death sat at the heart of every idea postulated by the group as they searched to discover the meaning behind the leader's dirt sketches. What did the six suns represent? What message was the Isconahua leader attempting to convey?

From the time of Alejo's death until the evening sunset, the nervous captives waited anxiously for the army to implement whatever action the leader's drawings required. Instead, the day passed without incident, the Isconahua carrying out their normal routines, seemingly unaffected by the morning execution. The lack of attention by the village eased the group's fears. They began to believe that the drawings did not prescribe any inevitable action.

"Maybe it's all just some sort of warning not to try to escape," Memphis suggested after the village life settled down for the night. "Perhaps they're just using Alejo and his escape attempt as an example."

The thought strangely comforted the women. Although the idea of no escape carried its own frightening implications, they saw that as a better alternative than sharing Alejo's fate. Abigail silently praised God for the evening darkness, which hid Alejo's body from their sight.

"Had Alejo ever tried to escape before?" Jonah asked Basil. Basil shook his head.

"Why then do you think he just took off all of a sudden last night?" Jonah asked.

"I cannot be sure," Basil said. "A week ago, though, he told me that he had awakened in the middle of the night and actually heard the guards snoring. He had spent the rest of the night trying to muster up the courage to run. Although he failed to find the nerve that evening, he told me that he had vowed never again to miss such an opportunity."

"It looks like he headed for the river," Memphis said.

"Yes," Basil replied. "There is a river that runs just past those trees. The Isconahua keep two dugout canoes tied to posts at the bank of the river. If one could reach the canoe, one would have a chance of escaping downriver."

While Memphis and Basil discussed the boats and river, Jonah snuggled on the floor with Grace. He held her close and kissed her softly. Soon they both fell asleep, as did Noah. Memphis ended his conversation with Basil and lay down beside Abigail. Accustomed to his jungle home and bed, Basil was the first to drift off to sleep. Six hours later, the rising sun and the naked army awakened them all.

The leader retraced his six suns in the dirt, which had lost some definition and clarity throughout the previous day and night. With the tip of his spear, he indicated the first sun and then lifted his spear and pointed at Basil.

Two soldiers entered the hut and picked up Basil by his weak arms. They led him out of the hut and threw him to the ground. Dirt filled Basil's beard. Completely detached, the Isconahua leader watched as Basil grasped to find his balance. Without hesitation, the leader plunged his spear into Basil's side. With one sweeping movement, he pulled the spear out and drove it in again, killing Basil Cosgrove.

Basil's body fell beside Alejo's. The army coldly followed the leader away from the hut. Abigail and Grace fell into the arms of the men, who closed around them protectively. The prisoners wept in shock and despair. As they mourned the latest death, Memphis began to pray aloud. Without hesitation, the others joined in as they sought the Lord's intervention in their desperate situation. Prayers for guidance, protection, and a miracle filled their minds and spirits.

When Jonah finally stepped out of the hut to clear his mind, he stopped to consider the sketches of the six suns. Looking at Basil and the first sun, the answer to the riddle became clear at last.

"I know what the six suns represent," he quietly said.

The others looked up at Jonah as he stood just outside the hut.

"What, Jonah?" Noah asked. "What do they mean?"

"They represent days," Jonah said. "And they represent us."

"Well, which is it, Jonah?" Noah asked.

"Both. Each sun is one day. So, there are six days. And each sun is one of us. There are...I mean, were, six of us."

Memphis reached the conclusion faster than Jonah could lead them there. He dropped his head and began to weep again. Jonah continued to explain his theory.

"I think that the leader of the men is trying to tell us that he is going to kill one of us every day for six days until we are all dead," Jonah solemnly said.

"I think Jonah's right," Noah said. "Remember, he pointed to the first sun and then pointed to Basil first of our group. Then, on the first day, they killed Basil."

Following Noah's assessment, all five of the prisoners arrived at the same question.

"Who did he point to secondly?" Jonah asked.

No one said anything. Everyone looked at one another trying to remember. At the time, the leader's signals did not seem exceedingly important. To whom did he assign the second sun, they all wondered. Memphis's tears overflowed. His head lower than ever, he addressed the group.

"Abigail," he whispered in a choked voice. "He pointed to Abigail next."

Memphis threw his arms around his wife and pulled her against his chest. Jonah searched for the right thing to say but found no appropriate words. No consolation sufficient, the day passed with little conversation. All around the hut, silent prayers were faithfully lifted up. It was not until late afternoon that Memphis finally spoke to the group and, when he did, he spoke boldly.

"Abigail and I are going to try to make it to the river tonight," he said.

Jonah, Grace, and Noah yielded him their full attention.

"I can't sit here and wait for the men to show up tomorrow and just hope that we're wrong about the six suns," Memphis said. "Because if we were right...well, then, they're going to kill my wife tomorrow morning."

Memphis and Abigail began to weep. Grace quickly followed.

"So, when the guards leave us tonight, I'm going to take Abigail out the back of this hut and run toward the river," Memphis continued. "And I think that we should all go together."

"It's risky," Noah said.

"Yes, but if we just sit here, they will certainly kill us, one at a time," Jonah said. "I say we try to escape."

"I agree," Grace said.

"If we all go, then I'm in, too," Noah said.

Memphis proceeded to outline the plan for the group. They would leave an hour after the rest of the village went to sleep. Jonah would lead the group out of the hut, through the brush and down to the riverbank. Memphis assigned himself to bring up the rear of the caravan. With Noah in front of him and the women just behind Jonah, Memphis felt that he had placed Abigail and Grace in the most secure position. Once they reached the river, Jonah would help the women into the canoe while Memphis untied the rope. Then, all five would flee for their lives.

CHAPTER 38

*I*N the Peruvian Amazon jungle, the majority of sunsets display an array of colors sporadically smudged across the sky. Rarely do the clouds effectively block the painted lights. Once the hue of the descending sun fades into the night, a full firmament of luminescent and brilliant stars manifest themselves replacing the previous sunset colors. On the night of the escape, however, thick rain clouds took over the sky, concealing all colors and stars. Minutes after the community residents fell asleep, the rain clouds burst and the storm began.

Memphis eyed the direction of the guards but could not see anyone for the thick sheets of rain coming down. Rain leaked through the old leaf roof of their hut, dousing all five of them. Though soaking wet, no one complained, as none of the prisoners intended to sleep that night anyway. An hour after the storm arrived, Memphis gave the signal.

"It's time," he said calmly.

Jonah grabbed Grace's hand as he stood.

"Stay close," he instructed her. To the rest he said quietly, "May God be with us."

Grace and Abigail followed Jonah out of the back of the hut. Noah and Memphis exited last. Jonah headed straight through the brush, following the sound of the current. Aside from becoming drenched by the slanted, driving, cold rain, the group moved unimpeded for the first five minutes. Grace stayed right behind Jonah who aggressively pushed through the overhanging branches without ever slowing down. Their initial pace gained speed with every step, as their hope of escape increased.

The sound of the rushing river current became louder than the rain as they edged closer and closer to the waiting canoes. Simultaneously with Jonah's thought that they would indeed make it, however, came the shouting of men from the village. Startled, Jonah stopped running.

"What was that?" he asked.

Memphis looked uphill toward the village. The shouting continued as more voices joined in. He waited a second longer. The shouting gradually became louder.

"They're coming!" he yelled.

Jonah took off. He pulled Grace as fast as she was able to keep up. Five pairs of feet tossed dirt and loose sticks in the air, the rain bouncing off their soaked heads. Dozens of bare feet followed in pursuit.

Familiar with their own backyard and assuming that the prisoners were headed toward the river, the Isconahua pursued the escapees from multiple angles.

"I see the river!" Jonah cried out. "I see the river!"

"There's the boat!" Grace screamed.

Jonah turned to his right and stumbled down the riverbank toward a long dugout canoe tied up by the bank. The plan was simple: he would aid the women in getting into the boat while Memphis untied the rope.

Mixed with the falling rain, the river water felt especially cold. Jonah waded in waist deep right away. He effortlessly slung Grace into the canoe. Taking Abigail's hand, he secured her as well. Parties of Isconahua warriors shouted as they neared the bank. Jonah turned and saw the leader sprinting, his spear lifted high.

"Hurry, Memphis!" Jonah shouted from the river.

"Get in!" Memphis shouted back.

Jonah climbed into the back of the canoe, motioning with his hand for his brother to get in. Noah splashed into the river and then pulled himself into the canoe. Memphis stopped at the post buried in the muddy bank. He frantically worked at his task of untying the rope. In record time, he loosened the line and moved toward the river.

An Isconahua warrior fired a long arrow from the base of the bank. It punctured Memphis in his right calf, sending him to the ground.

"Memphis!" Abigail screamed.

Memphis turned to see a dozen native men closing in on him. All bore bows and arrows or spears, and all raced toward him from less than twenty yards away. He looked back toward

Abigail and the boat. He lay a few feet from the river and even further from the canoe.

Memphis broke the long end of the arrow off, yelling from the pain. Blood poured down his wet leg. Using all of his strength, he stood to his feet and dove into the river. Coming out of the water, his hand grabbed the edge of the boat. Another arrow cut through the rain and entered Memphis's back, exiting through his chest. Memphis let out a scream of terror and pain.

"No!" Abigail shrieked. "Memphis!"

Abigail lunged toward the back of the canoe to grab Memphis.

"Abigail, don't!" Noah yelled.

Noah threw his body in front of Abigail just in time to absorb a third Isconahua arrow in his chest. The shot killed Noah instantly, knocking him out of the boat. Three warriors reached the river as Memphis was gasping for his final breaths. Seeing the advancing men, he mustered all of his strength to pull the canoe toward him and then sent it mightily out into the strong current. The current caught the dugout and swept it away from the arriving army.

Jonah dived to the back of the boat hoping to clasp Memphis's hand. Unable to do so, he hopelessly watched as Memphis sank into the river. The boat escaped the final, desperate shots of the Isconahua. A moment later, Jonah could no longer see his brother's body floating in the river.

Jonah, Grace, and Abigail fell into each other's arms, sobbing uncontrollably. They were completely unified in their shock and indescribable grief. In time, the shouts of the Isconahua disappeared with the rain. Images of Noah's and Memphis's final moments became permanently etched in Jonah's mind and he realized, with a stirring of recognition in his spirit, that they would not have escaped if Memphis had not placed himself between them and the Isconahua. Memphis had willingly laid down his life for his friends.

The three survivors wept for hours until they were left emotionally drained. At sunrise, Jonah, with a heavy heart, climbed into the back of the boat, picked up the oar, and began to row downriver.

PART THREE

Downriver

CHAPTER 39

THE December snow had settled into familiar blankets in its usual spot, covering the ground and the roof of the aging log cabin as the only Christmas decoration adorning the only home on this lonely Colorado hillside. Deer slipped through the edges of the nearby forest unnoticed. The whinny of a horse rang out clear in the crisp morning air, while two chickadees at the feeder outside the kitchen window seemed to shake for the season's chill.

The winter wind penetrated the slits in the window seals, challenging the wood stove that struggled to warm the single resident of the cabin.

Jonah closed the Bible he had been reading and filled a mug with the freshly brewed coffee, warming his elderly hands on the cup before taking his first sip of the morning. He coupled his drink with two different pills his doctor assured him would relieve the stiff pain in his knees as well as the arthritis in his hands. He paced from one end of the house to the other, pausing by the living room door in order to stare out the glass door just long enough to appreciate the beauty of the towering, snow-covered mountains watching over his humble cabin from across the twenty-acre field that was his front lawn.

It had been eight years since he and Grace had first moved to the foothills of the Sawatch Mountains. At the time, her health, though respectable for a 70-year-old grandmother, required the globetrotting couple to put an end to their traveling and settle down. Grace took time off from her photography – time off that proved indefinite – and even Jonah decided not to write until her health improved.

When she had passed away five years later, Jonah continued to shy away from writing as he struggled to adjust to life alone. Publishing a book seemed a trivial pursuit in light of losing the love of his life. He simply didn't care anymore.

Now, three years after Grace's death, a lonely Christmas Eve morning found Jonah ready to write.

He walked slowly past his bookcase running his fingers across the bindings of more than two-dozen books, bestsellers that he had written throughout the years, one of which had claimed the Pulitzer. His collection included twenty-six novels and one biography of the late Memphis Jones.

Sitting down at his desk, Jonah logged onto his computer, taking another sip of coffee as he waited for the startup screen to load. A weathered cigar box caught his eye. Placing the mug on the desk, Jonah picked up the box and, with emotion held in check, lifted the lid.

The box contained a collection of old letters from the two most important women of Jonah's adult life, Grace Cervantes Frost and Abigail Jones. He thumbed through the stack before picking up the latest addition, what had turned out to be the last letter of the priceless collection.

Postmarked a mere two months earlier, the letter bore a foreign return address that Jonah had memorized long ago: Kantchari, Burkina Faso, Africa. After Memphis's death, Abigail had continued to serve as a missionary throughout South America, Asia, and Africa. Her last place of residence was a small village located in the African bush just outside of Kantchari.

More than a few tears streamed out of Jonah's eyes, rolling over his wrinkled face before dropping onto Abigail's letter. Jonah read the letter aloud.

My dear Jonah,

It has been too long since our last hug. Oh, how I do miss you! No matter the depth of the friendships with which God has blessed me here, I am always left wanting as a bit of something seems to be missing. There are not many in the world who can connect with me as you can, for only two people in the world shared with me the experiences with the Amarakaeri and Isconahua—experiences that changed everything.

You were with me during my last days with Memphis, and I was with you during your final days with Noah, just as I was throughout Grace's sick years. Our bond is eternal.

I do hope to come and see you this Christmas. It has been nearly three years since my last visit to the States and I am due a hot bath and some English conversation. If you will build the fire, I'll heat up some hot chocolate so that we can sit in comfort and re-tell our favorite stories about your lovely Grace and my brave Memphis as we watch the falling snow decorate your front porch.

How are your children and grandchildren? Thank you for the pictures of your Memphis and Noah and their families. They both turned out to be handsome men and wonderful fathers. You must be very proud of them. I know that Grace always was. I loved seeing her face light up whenever she spoke about your sons.

I hope you will come for a visit. The people here haven't stopped asking about you ever since your two-week stay a couple of years ago. Oh, what Memphis would have given to see you serving as a missionary with the people here! How he would have rejoiced to know that you now follow the Jesus he lived for! The Jesus he died for. I know that he's waiting to celebrate it all with you one day when you two meet again.

Do you get out much? You mentioned in your last letter that you were considering spending Christmas with the boys and their families in Michigan if you were able to finish the first few chapters in your new book. Did you write? Are you going to Michigan? You should go. Writing isn't everything, you know.

Well, it looks like a heavy rainstorm is on the horizon. I need to get these pages covered and gather my laundry from the clothesline. I hope this letter finds you well. Please write as soon as you can.

With love,

Abigail

Six weeks after Jonah had received the letter, he learned that Abigail had passed away. She was buried in Kantchari, Africa.

Jonah tried to fold the letter and return it to its envelope, but streaming tears blinded him. He dropped the open letter into the box and covered his face with his shaking hands.

"They're gone," he cried out. "They're all gone."

Jonah looked at the framed pictures on his desk. The one that Grace had taken of Memphis, Noah, and Jonah by the riverbank of the Amarakaeri village, moments before the Isconahua attacked, only brought more tears. Jonah took the picture in his hands, trying desperately to remember what the moment had felt like, trying desperately to feel that way again.

Another picture, of Grace and Jonah on their second vacation to Rome, caught his eye next.

"She was so beautiful," he said to himself, his lips quivering.

After a few minutes passed, Jonah regrouped, returning the pictures to their places. Opening a new document on his computer, he allowed his arthritic fingers to settle in on the home row of his keyboard. Staring at the blank screen, two more minutes passed.

Jonah looked at the third picture on his desk, one taken last spring – his sons, Memphis and Noah, and their families crowded together on a park bench. The grandchildren seemed to smile only for Jonah, as if no one else was ever meant to see the picture. Jonah smiled back at them, picturing them celebrating Christmas together in the snow at Memphis's home in Michigan.

A spontaneous idea leapt into his mind.

"Oh, how surprised they would all be!" Jonah laughed to himself as he considered the possibility.

Before he could second-guess himself, Jonah shut down the computer, hurriedly threw a few items of clothing into a small suitcase, and grabbed Grace's camera as he headed for the door. He pulled on the first coat he saw on the rack by the front porch and threw on his favorite winter hat as well. Breathing in the morning chill as he locked the door behind him, a smile no one had seen in quite some time enveloped his face.

"Today, I will live," he declared. "Tomorrow, I will write."

About the Author

PHOTO BY BRIAN WILLIAMS

JONATHAN WILLIAMS served as a missionary with the International Mission Board's Xtreme Team in the jungles of Peru for two years. It was there, lying under a mosquito net in a hut in the middle of the Amazon jungle, that Williams began to write his first novel, *Jungle Sunrise.* Living with a previously unreached indigenous tribe, the Amarakaeri, Williams experienced firsthand the beauty and danger of native life as he had the opportunity to share the Gospel of Jesus Christ, hunt with bows and arrows, fish with spears, navigate rivers, and encounter every aspect of the tribe's culture. This breathtaking Amazon scene serves as the backdrop for *Jungle Sunrise.*

Williams, twenty-nine, writes and lives in North Texas with his wife, Jessica, where he pastors Body Life Church as he pursues a Masters of Divinity degree from Southwestern Baptist Theological Seminary. His passion and desire is to inspire readers with creativity and truth.

Write him at PeruMission@hotmail.com.

Acknowledgments

WHILE it may take a village to raise a child, it takes two villages to publish a book. Fortunately, I'm a member of some pretty encouraging tribes.

Without my beautiful bride, Jessica, I could have never finished this novel or persevered through the journey. Thank you for believing in the story from the beginning, reading it in a day, and even naming the book. Your affirmation throughout was incomparable, and your inspiration, indispensable.

Dad, your initial edits and influence tremendously strengthened the caliber of the book. Mom, your encouragement and early read of the novel gave further resolve to my desire to share this story with others. I also want to thank Brian, Brooke, Joey, Nicole, Jack, and Sue for their preliminary reads and enduring support.

To my agent, Abe Arias, thank you for championing this book for so long. You are an answer to many prayers. To Michele Arias, I am forever grateful to you as you advocated Jonah & Memphis' story, convincing Abe to read it.

Mr. Gerald Nordskog, I admire your commitment to publish Noble Novels and am honored to be a part of the Nordskog team. Thank you for giving this book a chance, and thanks to the entire Nordskog Publishing family, especially Desta Garrett and Kimberley Woods, who invested themselves in breathing life into this novel.

Acknowledgments

I am thankful to the Xtreme Team, my partners in the Gospel. Living the mission with you was one of the greatest adventures I've known. I also want to express my heartfelt gratitude to the Amarakaeri churches, villages, and families. Thank you for allowing me to share life and the Gospel with you, and for shaping this story when you unveiled your wildly beautiful native culture. *Dakiti.*

Finally, I praise God for blessing me with Body Life Church, relatives, and friends who faithfully prayed for this moment. Thank you all. Enjoy the story.

– Jonathan Williams
Christmas 2009, Ft. Worth, Texas

Publisher's Word

The Great Commission:
All authority has been given to Me in heaven and on earth.
Go therefore and make disciples of all the nations, baptizing them
in the name of the Father and of the Son and of the Holy Spirit,
teaching them to observe all things that I have commanded you;
and lo, I am with you always, even to the end of the age.
(Matthew 28:18-20, NKJV)

WE are pleased to present *Jungle Sunrise* as Nord-skog Publishing's third fiction book in our series of Noble Novels! Man's imagination can be a marvelous gift of God as it is employed in fiction storytelling, not just to entertain but to enlighten and inspire readers.

The Lord's Great Commission is always a worthy Christian focus. Our part, to publish peace and salvation (Isaiah 52:7), is enriched by bringing to you a Christian missions adventure – fiction, but authentically rooted in the author's experience in the field.

When a creative writer manages – in history, biography, or even a fiction story – to impart to us a virtual sense of the transforming power of Christ to redeem a human life, we believe the Lord is glorified, readers edified, and workers may be encouraged to fulfill His Great Commission.

We believe that godly writers are amongst God's gifted artisans, doing their best to present themselves to God as one approved, a worker who does not need to be ashamed, rightly dividing the word of truth (2 Timothy 2:15). Writers, insofar as they glorify the Lord with their words, are craftsmen not unlike those called to create the sacred furnishings of Moses' tabernacle: "See, I have called by name Bezalel…. And I have filled him with the Spirit of God, in wisdom, and understanding, in knowledge, and in all manner of workmanship…. [And] put in his heart the ability to teach" (Exodus 31:2, 35:34, NKJV).

The author Jonathan Williams is a pastor but for two years he was an Xtreme Team missionary living deep in the Peruvian jungle with indigenous tribes. The characters in this story are fictitious, but you will find them vital and reflective of a remote mission-field experience. They include a missionary couple, a linguist, a photo-journalist, and an anthropologist, along with the boatman they hire and several tribes of natives. Into this mix is cast the main character, Jonah, whose life is falling apart, leaving him at the extreme end of his rope. Dragged on this adventure by his linguist brother, we see him first as a New York City college professor slipping into depression, to a man outside his element learning the ropes of the Amazon jungle, and then suddenly stumbling into a situation that could likely

lead to his imminent death.

The author gives us an intimate glimpse of lives being transformed by the Gospel. So enter this jungle adventure, but know you will find it hard to put this book down!

– Gerald Christian Nordskog
PUBLISHER

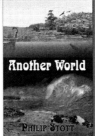
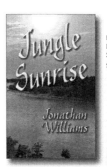

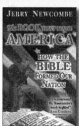

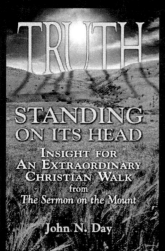

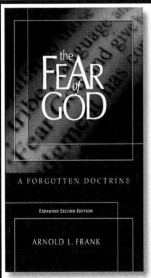